Minot Judson Savage

Bluffton

A story of to-day

Minot Judson Savage

Bluffton
A story of to-day

ISBN/EAN: 9783744748100

Printed in Europe, USA, Canada, Australia, Japan

Cover: Foto ©Andreas Hilbeck / pixelio.de

More available books at **www.hansebooks.com**

BLUFFTON:

A STORY OF TO-DAY.

.

BY

M. J. SAVAGE.

———◆———

THIRD EDITION.

BOSTON:
GEO. H. ELLIS, 141 FRANKLIN STREET.
1889.

NOTE.

THE incidents of this story are chiefly facts. This is specially true of those things that may to some readers appear forced or exaggerated. The facts, however, do not all belong to any one place, nor to the experience of any one person.

The people who live in Bluffton will doubtless recognize some touches of local scenery; but, if they look to find the *characters* among their friends and neighbors, they will most certainly be mistaken.

By bringing out in strong relief some of the evils of one phase of religion, and some of the good of the opposite, the writer would not be understood to assert that the evil is all on one side and the good all on the other. He has simply emphasized those things that were essential to his present purpose. Good and evil are both *human*, and not confined to any one religious type.

MAY, 1878.   3

CONTENTS.

BLUFFTON:

A STORY OF TO-DAY.

I.

AT THE LEVEE.

"WHY do you call it Maple City?" said Mark, as, after an hour's walk about the town, he and his friend Tom were slowly strolling down the street — cut through the bluff — that led to the levee.

"Oh! I don't know," replied Tom, "unless it may be for the reason that the place isn't a city, and hasn't a maple-tree in its limits. As for the matter of names, you know all the towns East have a Spruce Street, and a Pine Street, and generally there isn't a spruce or a pine in sight. Perhaps the mental suggestion has some shade and comfort in it."

"And as for your cities, Tom, I understand that all cross-roads are cities out here."

"Yes," said he, "just as the peddler shouted 'Hot pies!' because that was 'what they called 'em.' They name towns here on the same principle that mothers christen their children George Washington and Napoleon Bonaparte, — seem-

7

ing to have the notion that the quality of the name will somehow *strike in*, and make Congressmen out of 'em some day."

"Towns grow so fast," replied Mark, "that I suppose they want the name big enough to cover the future. Now, I am assured by the committee from Bluffton that the place will at least double in five years. And if they get the Great Central Railroad, for which this and all the neighboring places are fighting, they will even double on that."

"'They all do it,'" drolly replied Tom. "All the places are going to double in three to five years. But, if some of them don't 'flat out' on their expectations, they'll have to import the inhabitants of the neighboring planets to furnish people enough. And then, as to railroads, they seem to overlook one thing, — that it is just as easy to get *out* of town on a new road as it is to get *in*, and that people may leave as well as come."

"But, at any rate," said Mark, "it indicates the young blood, the vigor, the hope, of a great nation whose life is ahead, a prophecy, and not a page in history illustrated by ruins. A burly, growing boy is always extravagant: he always wants the biggest boots and trousers he can get, because he feels the undeveloped man in him, and wants to appear like one. Little old men I never took to anyhow. The boy who is forty years old at thirteen will be too tame for usefulness by the time he is thirty, and ought to be buried at thirty-five. So I say, Hail to the awkward but irrepressible vigor of the New West."

"Well," said Tom, "you've made your peroration just in

time ; for there is the smoke of the steamer rising just over the point yonder, and you'll hear your first Mississippi whistle in a moment."

The two young men now stood on the levee. The Rev. Mark Forrest, after a year or two of outpost duty, now, at the age of twenty-five, was on his way to take charge of an evangelical church at Bluffton, a "city" some miles farther down the river. Tom was an old school-friend, five years his senior, who, taking to business, had gone West, made and lost one or two fortunes, married, and with his Western wife and two bright children, was now living at Maple City. Mark, who had never seen the Mississippi before, had telegraphed his friend to meet him for the hour between the arrival of the train and the time for the steamer on her down trip. He had met the church committee in the East, and, after consultation, had consented to go out like Abraham, "not knowing whither he went." And here he was so far on his way. His trunk and small library had been sent on by express, so that he stood with only his travelling-bag in his hand. As it was Saturday, and he must preach his first sermon to his new people on the following day, he could only pay his friend this flying visit on the way. They could now, being so near each other, tie up the broken threads of their old intimacy at their leisure.

And now the steamer, rounding the headland, swept into full view, at the same time sending out an unearthly scream, as if to strike terror into the heart of the western wilds, and give the woods warning of the speedy approach of the railroad and the steam-plough. To Mark, who had seen only

ocean-steamers before, she was a new sensation. A tall pole
tipped with a gilded ball rose into the air from the extreme
end of her bow; two smoke-stacks, high above every thing
else, belched out enormous volumes of black, soft-coal
smoke, that floated lazily on the still, bright June air; a
black mass of men, relieved by the gayer colors of the
women, crowded forward on the shoreward side. She looked
all decks and cabins and saloons; while the bow end of her
low hulk was piled up with bales and boxes and barrels,
sprinkled all over which were the tow-colored rags and
ebony faces of the " roustabouts," whose business it was to
" tote " the freight aboard and ashore.

"Well, what do you think of her, Mark?" said Tom.

" I think," replied Mark, " that a party of friends on an
outdoor boat like this, floating on such a glassy river, and
through such a perfect air, and under such a soft sky, drifting
on through sweeps of wide prairie, and along dark woods,
and past bright young towns, might easily fancy themselves
to have found the ' earthly paradise ' with modern improve-
ments. As I'm in no hurry to get aboard, let's stand here,
and see the people, and the process of landing."

The steamer now headed in toward the shore, and, with a
grating noise on the bottom, ran her " nose " against the
levee. The river-current caught the stern, and slowly swung
her round until she rested quartering on the bank, and
headed up stream. And now, as the planks were run out,
belated hacks came tearing down the streets, carts rattled
over the stones, and numberless " men and brothers " yelled
on their bony steeds attached to their two-wheeled drays;

and others came with trunks, boxes, or casks on their shoulders, from the warehouses or the neighboring station. But, above all the noise of the crowd, one sound caught and fixed the attention of Mark : it was the stupendous swearing of the mate. He had witnessed displays of profanity before, so elaborate as to entitle them to rank as works of art ; but as he stood here, and saw him pile Ossa upon Pelion, beheld "Alps on Alps arise," and looked down into yawning gulfs of blasphemy, it seemed to him that here was a Titan playing with the gigantic upheavals of language, while ordinary men only walked along on the commonplace flats of the dictionary. Of course he was shocked ; but, while he was one who shrunk from every touch of irreverence, his sense of the ludicrous was so developed that sometimes the absurdity of a thing made him forget, for the time, its wickedness. Turning to Tom, he said, —

"Is that a specimen of Western ability in the profanity line ? "

"Yes," he replied with a shade of irony in his tone : " in this glorious Western world you must expect to find the proportions of things maintained. The man, you see, is ambitious to have his swearing on the same magnificent scale as our ' mighty ' rivers and our ' boundless ' prairies."

"But do they all swear like that? Listen now ! It rattles through the clouds of his words like the jerk and crash of lightning in a thunder-storm."

"All the mates do," Tom replied : " it seems to be their special business to swear at the deck-hands. They hurl oaths at them as if they were stones, and crack them over the back with a sharp phrase as if it were the sting of a lash. They get so used to it, that I doubt if they would move at all if they were spoken to in ordinary language. They are like the old man's oxen that we used to laugh about. You know they got so used to being sworn at, that, when the old fellow was converted, the only way he could get them along was to sit on the cross-board, and shout at them profane-sounding selections from the New Testament. So these fellows would 'slow up' till you couldn't see them move, if he didn't swear all the time."

But just here Mark's eye caught sight of some one going up the plank, and in an instant the mate was forgotten.

"Tom," he said, "I'm in luck. There goes old Judge Hartley. Now, you see, I'm in for good company down the river."

"Judge Hartley," said Tom : "what brings him out here?"

"Oh! I forgot to tell you that he has sold out East, and is moving to Bluffton. He's going to be in my church."

"Then I pity you," growled Tom.

"Why?" briefly inquired Mark.

"Why? Don't you remember how in the old church at home he was always on the scent for heresy? He even suspected the old minister's soundness in the faith. And now let me warn you beforehand, that, if you happen to learn any thing that hasn't been in the old 'Bodies of Divinity' long enough to get rusty, he'll make it hot for you."

"Oh! but you're too hard on him, Tom," answered Mark. "He's just my idea of a typical Puritan; neither better nor worse. He's sunny and sweet and kind in his home. But all his natural tenderness has been laid on what he thinks the altar of God. So it is a matter of duty with him to hate and fight any departures from orthodoxy. He's of the stuff of which martyrs are made ; and, being ready himself to die for God's truth, his sense of duty would stifle all tenderness toward one that he looked upon as an enemy of divine revelation. But he'll broaden a little out here, and we'll get on capitally."

"Well, I hope so," said Tom. "But who was that young lady that followed the judge up the plank?"

"I don't know," replied Mark, "unless it is one of his daughters. I haven't seen them since they were girls."

"Whoever it is, hurry up, Mark, for they are taking in the plank. Perhaps you'll find light enough in the daughter to relieve the sombreness of the old judge."

"Haven't time to think of those things yet," said Mark. "But good-by : I'll write after Sunday."

So saying, he leaped aboard. The bell had ceased ringing, and the boat swung off into the river. He stood a minute on the lower deck, as she swept out into the current ; and then went up the gangway to find the judge.

Judge Hartley was a tall, close-shaven, gray-eyed man of sixty. Having once been a probate judge, the title still remained. Retired from active business with a competency, he had decided to move West, and make his future home near the residence of his only surviving brother.

II.

ON THE STEAMER.

MARK really thought — and no wonder; for older and wiser men have done the same before him — that his head and heart were too full of other things to have any room in them for love. He was going to study; he was going to travel; he was going to test himself, and find out what was in him and what he could do, and so make himself a permanent footing somewhere, — before he allowed himself to think of a home. He would make himself and his position a worthy gift before he would presume to offer them to such a woman as he would love. He had not yet learned, that, though "marriages of convenience" are always in order, real love does not come at a beck, nor wait to be sent for. He knew not as yet that no head nor heart can be crammed so full but that love will find himself a place, and come in even though the doors are shut.

So, while he looked after the judge, he found the beginning of a pain that would not let him rest, and that yet he would not have been free from for all the study and travel and ambitions of which he had dreamed since boyhood. While he thought he was only walking a common plank-deck, he, in

reality, stumbled across the threshold and through the gate-
way of an enchanted "castle in Spain," where he was to
find dungeons of darkness, and instruments of exquisite
torture, as well as galleries of pictures, halls of song, and
lofty towers of vision.

Stepping into the saloon long enough to register his name,
pay his fare, and leave his satchel at the office, he passed
out on to the forward deck. Leaning against the starboard
rail, he stopped entranced with the beauty of the scene ; for
it seemed to him that he had walked into a waking dream.
It was about four o'clock in the afternoon. The right bank
of the river was a continuous wood-crowned bluff. The
river itself at this point curved south-east, so that the sun
seemed caught in the ragged tops of the trees straight
ahead. What would have been its unbearable brightness in
the open sky was broken into a golden mist and spray
among the branches, as sometimes the falling waters of a cas-
cade are turned into a sort of impalpable cloud of glory by
jagged rocks and the height of their fall. The river was a
veritable "sea of glass." The air was mellow and soft, and
spread over the scene a saffron-colored haze that seemed
the stuff of which dreams are made. For the moment
every thing was still save the distant murmur of voices and
the plash of the paddle-wheels, that only seemed to deepen
the silence.

The steamer drifted so softly that it was almost like floating in air. There was in his mind a curious blending of
memory and anticipation. His home, his childhood, and
his old life were behind ; and he was drifting on into a future

of unspeakable glory.   This was the Mississippi, and around
him was a new world.   He was in the boat of De Soto; and
just around that headland yonder would spring into view the
fadeless beauty of the " earthly paradise " that the eager
Spanish eyes so looked for in this strange, far-off land.   And
these fancies melted into the visions of the seer of Patmos.
The river of life, and the mystic trees, and the sea of
crystal, and the blinding glory, were blended with the
landscape.   He gazed straight on into the light; and with
his eyes half closed, and lost in thought, the illusion was
complete.   Had a traditional Bible angel floated silently
across the glory, he would hardly have roused from his brief
revery; for it would have been a part of his dream.   But
what he did see startled him into a confused self-conscious-
ness.   Turning his head a little, as he became aware of a
presence near him, he found himself looking straight into
the face of what seemed to him the most beautiful girl he
had ever looked upon.   He had read of such in poem and
romance; but he had never yet believed that there was in
flesh and blood a face and form like this.   In one rapid
glance, — in less time than it takes to tell it, — he took in
the fact that her figure was faultless, her dress so perfect as
to be forgotten, her face oval in shape and brunette in com-
plexion.   Her heavy masses of hair were black, as were the
long lashes that shaded her eyes; and her eyes themselves
were liquid and deep, like the bottomless lakes that lie tree-
fringed at the feet of lofty mountains.

He had only time to note these particulars, and to accuse
himself of rudeness for thus staring in the face of a stran-

ger, when, in a voice that betrayed only girlish unconsciousness and the frank simplicity of a guileless nature, she said, —

"Isn't this Mr. Forrest?"

There was a moment of confusion before he could fully
believe that this human angel, that had so suddenly stepped
out of his vision of glory, had really spoken to him ; but,
seeing her look frankly in his face for reply, he answered, —

"Certainly, that is my name ; but you must pardon me if
I do not remember you. I have never seen a face " — " so
beautiful as yours," he just saved himself from saying ; and
finished not very elegantly, by adding — "like yours."

She recognized the broken and awkward phrase by a
quizzical look, which soon passed, leaving only her simple
unconsciousness once more, and added, —

"Why, I thought you would know me. Have I really
changed so much in six years? I am Margaret Hartley.
You used to call me Madge when I was a little girl."

"You really must forgive me for forgetting you," said he.
"I was in a day-dream when I first caught sight of your
face. If you hadn't spoken, I fear I should have taken you
for a part of my vision ; but, indeed, you have changed from
the fly-away Madge I knew at school."

"Not for the worse, I hope," said she ; and then, without
waiting for the reply that she knew courtesy at least would
make complimentary, she continued, —

"Perhaps I recognized you the more readily because
father and I have been speaking of you. We knew to-morrow was to be your first Sunday in Bluffton, and we were
wondering what sort of minister you had grown to be. We
are to be of your flock, you know."

"Yes: I had heard that you were moving West; and, indeed, as I stood on the levee at Maple City, I saw your father go up the plank, but, not seeing your face, I did not recognize you as the one who was with him."

"Mother is dead, you know; and the other girls we have left in Chicago with aunt, until we get the house ready to receive them. I am the housekeeper now. But father must be wondering what has become of me. Don't you want to see him?"

"Of course I do. It was he I had started to find when the wonder of this new river scenery threw me into the day-dream in which your face appeared. I was more glad than I can tell when I saw him; for I did not like to enter on my new field alone. It will make the strange church seem like home to see his face among the pews. Where have you left him?"

"Aft, I believe the sailors call it: on the deck at the rear of the saloon. I had been at my stateroom for a moment, and strayed this way, on coming out, to take a look down the river. I have visited here before, and the scenery seems like an old acquaintance. Uncle James lives at Bluffton, you know."

This was said as they walked together down the saloon. There was a friendly, old-time greeting on the part of Mr. Forrest and Judge Hartley. And, drawing three camp-stools together, they sat down and talked over the past, and went over the causes that brought them all out to their new Western home.

The boat glided onward, opening up behind them an

ever-changing panorama of loveliness. Now a bluff stood out boldly, and with its rocky front looked down upon them as they drifted through its shadows. On the other shore, the prairie stretched off for miles, till a range of hills, tipped with the rays of the slanting sun, closed in the horizon. Then a green valley, down which a tree-shaded creek ran darkly in the deepening shadow, wound off and up, and hid itself in the mystery of the hills. And here and there were islands that were emeralds set in crystal.

Pointing out to each other the beauties of scenery as they passed, they fell to talking of their coming life and work.

"This Western country is grand and wonderful," said the judge. " But I imagine that, religiously, it is not much like New England. There is a little colony of the Puritan element at Bluffton ; and we must try to be like the leaven of the Scriptures, and see if we can't bring them to our New-England ways."

"I have only seen two or three of the people," answered Mr. Forrest, "and do not know much about the rest of the inhabitants."

"I'm afraid they're a godless set," replied the judge. " My brother writes me, that it is a sabbath-breaking, horse-racing, drinking place, not much like the God-fearing town we are used to."

"We must show them a better style of morals, then," said Mr. Forrest.

"Morals !" rather emphatically exclaimed the judge. "Morals are good enough as far as they go ; but they need something deeper than that. Morals never yet saved a town any more than an individual. It's the gospel they need, — the pure, unadulterated gospel; and I hope that you are ready to preach it to them fearlessly, Mr. Forrest."

"I trust," modestly replied he, "that I shall be able to preach God's truth to them, and help them mend their ways."

"Good, hard doctrine," continued the judge, "the wrath of God against sin, the 'sincere milk of the word,' salvation only through the atoning blood, — that is what they need."

"We must expect," he replied, "to find their ways different from ours. All new countries are rough at first. It's a lower type of civilization."

"Don't talk of 'civilization,' and 'different ways,'" said the judge. "Such words savor too strongly of worldly wisdom, and 'philosophy falsely so called.' Sin is the same thing, and comes from the same Devil, all the world over. We must be uncompromising. The strongholds of Satan's kingdom must be attacked by the 'sword of the Lord and of Gideon.'"

Mr. Forrest was as earnest in his faith, and thought himself as sound in his orthodoxy, as the judge. But, though he remembered the tone in his conversation that used to be so familiar in the old prayer-meeting talks at home, it had now a strange, far-away sound in his ears. He had become accustomed to put his religious meanings into the talk of every day, thinking it better to translate divine messages into the language of the street. So he was not sorry when Madge jumped to her feet, as the whistle blew its shrill blast, and said, —

"Come, father and Mr. Forrest, let's leave theology now, and see the steamer pass through the bridge."

They rose and hurried through the saloon, and stood together on the forward deck. They were just in time. The draw had swung to its place, and the quickening current, as it rushed between the piers, was bearing the steamer on with its rapid flow. The boat seemed to thrill with the lift of the waters; and she shot through the opening as if rejoicing in the intelligence and grace of motion of a living thing.

And now Bluffton itself was in sight, and the boat was all astir with the preparation for landing. They stood for a moment to take in the natural features of the town. Mark first noticed the tall bluff at its southern end, from which it took its name. Sheer up it rose a hundred and fifty feet, crowned with one lone tree on the edge of its summit, whose gnarled and crooked roots stretched out and curled down over its rocky face. A lower and irregular range of hills stretched round in a semicircle, bounding the horizon at the back of the town, and jutting out boldly again on the river-bank above the city in another bluff only less noticeable than the first. A stream ran through the city, dividing it irregularly into an upper and lower town. Its nearer side had all the dingy and ill-kept appearance that marks so many of these river-towns; but it looked very picturesque and beautiful as it stretched back from the river-front, and climbed past the open square and up to the tops of the hills that were brilliant with the glory of the setting sun.

The scene on the levee only repeated that at Maple City;

save that the judge and Margaret recognized and beckoned
to the friends that waited for them on shore.   Mr. Forrest
himself saw a member of the church committee that had
met him at the East, come to welcome him to his new field.
As they passed down the plank, he bade the judge a hearty
good-night, saying, —

"We shall meet again to-morrow."

And now for the first time, at parting, he took the hand
of Margaret, thrilled with the consciousness that it was no
longer a child's hand to be touched or dropped indifferently,
but the hand of a woman.   He had shaken the hands of a
thousand women before, and only regarded it as a formal
piece of ceremony.   But this soft touch tingled in his veins,
and throbbed wildly through his heart.   All pure, new love
has about it a sense of reverent awe.   So while he would not
have dared to hold her hand, or give it conscious pressure, a
new sense of loss came over him when it was withdrawn ;
and he trembled as he waked up to the fact that the power
of control over his own future happiness had passed out of
his hands, and now lay in the touch and look of one, who, so
far as he knew, was utterly indifferent to him except on the
one point as to whether she was going to like or dislike him
as a minister.

So, while he was driven to the hotel, he became aware that
Bluffton now had in it, for his weal or woe, something besides
a church.

III.

RETROSPECT.

AND now, while the young minister is resting from his journey, and preparing for the word he must speak to-morrow, and which is to strike the keynote to the work which he is to undertake in Bluffton, let us glance back a little, and see who and what kind of a man he is.

In person he was a little above the medium height, straight, broad-shouldered, and rather muscular in his build. His head was large, and covered with wavy, soft brown hair. His forehead was high and broad, and terminated at the base by cliffs of brows that reminded one of Tennyson's " bar of Michael Angelo ; " while beneath these were a pair of large gray eyes, set so deep that they looked smaller than they were, except when he was animated in private or roused in public speech. His nose was large, straight, and prominent. A long and firm upper-lip was completely concealed by a heavy moustache, with the exception of which his face was smooth. The face — which was strong and striking rather than handsome — was rounded by a chin no way remarkable, but only in keeping with the rest of his features. He dressed in accordance with the one canon of perfect taste that he

was always ready to advocate for both man and woman, —
so well and so simply that no one would think any thing
about the dress, but only notice and remember the person.

He had behind him such a memory of struggle and toil as
fitted him to understand, and brought him into keen and
ready sympathy with, all

"The low, sad music of humanity."

Born in poverty, a hard-working farmer's son, he kept ever
hanging in his study, as an ideal portrait of his remembered childhood, the picture of Whittier's "Barefoot Boy."
Many a time, sleeping up under the bare, sloping roof of
the little old brown farmhouse garret, while the wild winter
storm rocked and sung him to sleep, had he waked in the
morning to find a snowdrift sifted through the broken roof,
and lying across his bed. Rising, the winter through, at
four o'clock in the morning, to do his father's and the neighbors' "chores," and cut the wood for the day's fire, before the
time for school, he was used to trudging through the snow,
thin-clad, to the old district schoolhouse, and struggling
hard, or playing hard, to keep back the tears that the nip-
ping cold would extort.

He was strongly religious in his natural bent, and he was
nursed and trained in all the traditional views and ways of
orthodoxy. Dreaming from childhood of the work of Jesus
in Judæa, and of the still dark wastes of heathendom that
had not heard his name, he used to wonder why all men
were not ministers of his gospel; and he could not remember the time when he did not plan to be one himself.

He was cradled amid scenes of such idyllic country beauty as naturally gave an æsthetic and poetic turn to his sensitive mind. The farmhouse was on a hill-top overlooking a lovely river, that wound away past intervale and wood, till it lost itself in the hills that rose higher and higher northward in a range of mountains that closed in the horizon about the region of the lakes. A brook, the scene of childhood sports, of adventures of hunting and fishing, wound through the meadow, and poured its tiny tribute into the river at the foot of the hill.

He rummaged through the village library, and feasted on the wit, humor, and satire of the first series of the " Biglow Papers ; " he devoured Pope and Dryden and Cowley, and twice read through " Paradise Lost," long before he had any idea of general literature, or the rank to which these writers were entitled on the world's roll of fame. He also had the attack, — inevitable as teething, — to which all thoughtful children are subject, of verse-making himself. He wrote verse enough for a book by the time he was fifteen, which bashfulness perhaps, more than compassion for a suffering humanity, prevented his inflicting on a patient world.

Such were some of the salient outlines on the background of his memory.

At his first entry of the seminary for theological training, his reverence for professors and learned lecturers was such that he did little but receive and absorb their teachings. He even regarded as presumptuous the hardihood of some occasional student who dared to question the dictum of a master in divinity ; and he thought it was good enough for

him when a sharp retort and a "settler" took the place of
an explanation. A student asked Dr. Wayland, one day,
why divine inspiration was necessary for the writing of the
Book of Proverbs. The doctor crushed him by asking him
to go and write as good a chapter himself. At this time
Mark would have looked at such a rejoinder as conclusive.
He did not stop, till afterwards, to think that because "not
twenty men in Boston could have written Shakspeare," as a
critic once profoundly said, that hardly proved that Othello
was inspired and infallible.

But toward the latter part of his seminary-life he began to
use his own brain, and think for himself. Not, by any means,
that he questioned the system of orthodoxy, — very far from
it; but he began to feel, that, while such and such things
might be true, he could not preach as a mere echo of others'
thoughts. It must be *true to him* before he could dare to
speak it. Thus, without his knowing it, he admitted a principle fatal to his soundness, and that was to lead him a long
and weary and painful way.

He did not read or study outside of his system, except as
special books were pointed out to him; and these he was
taught to consider already abolished, or as profane quibblers
who chose "darkness rather than light," and were therefore
"given over to a reprobate mind." A perfect divine revelation had been given to men; and only the wilfully wicked
refused to see it. One prominent professor from Union
Seminary advised the students not to read any books later
than the seventeenth century. A prominent, successful D.D.
and pastor told them that the books that attacked their

system were weak, if not venomous, and they ought not to waste their time in reading them, but spend it in saving souls. Beside, Satan was able to make "the worse appear the better reason;" and since man was fallen, and the divine light blotted from his mind, to follow "profane and carnal reason" was chasing a will-o'-the-wisp that would lead them into the swamps of corruption, and endanger their souls' eternal welfare.

Through such influences he passed to his work. God was to be found only in the Bible as interpreted in the popular writings. Man was corrupt; nature was only to be used to illustrate revelation; and the great scientific thinkers of the world had lost their spiritual vision by long contact with a debasing materialism.

When his theological course was completed, he said to his chum, —

"If the rest of you choose to settle down in some little quiet nook, and wither into a petty routine, I do not. I'm off for the frontiers."

"But what will you get on the frontiers except rough work?" said his chum.

"I'll get a knowledge of humanity; I'll measure the size of the continent; I'll see how my theology works in practical life," said he. "Then, if I wish to settle East, I can labor in view of the whole field."

So off he went, by the way of the Isthmus, to California and Oregon. He went up and down the country, exploring the field, the wants of this place and that, and at last located in a mining-camp, and began preaching in schoolhouses and on the street-corners as he could get a hearing.

He learned one thing that was of infinite use to him in his after-life ; and that was, to stand strong on his own feet, and place the man before the minister. The "Rev." attached to his name, he soon found out, instead of giving him currency as sterling coin, was looked upon with suspicion as a surface indication of counterfeit and religious swindle. His being a minister, instead of being a proof of manhood, was rather against him. After he had proved himself a man, then they began, for the first time, to respect the minister. Not that they had any thing against ministers, as such ; they remembered home too well for that : but the title had so often been used to cloak a sham, that they wanted to know what was under a black coat. Wrecked and tumble-down ministers, with the manhood gone out, were scattered, like deserted and broken-roofed cabins, all through the mining-regions.

So after Mark had "cleaned out" some "roughs" that came in to break up his prayer-meeting; after he had knocked down a brute on the street for abusing a little boy ; when they found that he was always on the side of right, "meant business" as they said, and was always ready to "help a feller in trouble," — they "took to" him wonderfully. One rough old miner told him privately that "he didn't know but he liked him 'bout as well ez ef he warn't a minister." And he added, "Ef yer want any dust to help a boy whose mine has 'petered out,' an' who's got sick, jes' show yer hand, and I'm yer man. Or ef any shufflin' bilk interferes with your meetin's, I'll clean him out quicker'n greased lightnin'. Yer can count on me."

And another lesson he learned ; and that was, that when

dealing with men who cared nothing for traditions, who got right down to "hard-pan" on all questions, and who believed with their whole souls that it took just a hundred cents in gold to make a dollar, he must appeal to their common sense and reason, must talk home to their every-day life, or else he might as well not talk at all.

Along with this kind of life, he had read and studied widely and deeply as his time and means for purchasing books permitted; for he wished to be master of the problems of the day in the scholarly world, as well as master of the human heart in its every-day manifestations of common life.

When you stand by a river-bank, and know its source and general trend, you can with tolerable accuracy forecast its onward course, and tell into what ocean it will empty. So it was needful that so much of the past course of the young minister should be indicated, in order to a better understanding of what is to follow.

IV.

FIRST SUNDAY AT BLUFFTON.

BY eight o'clock on Sunday morning, Mr. Forrest had eaten a light breakfast, — the slight nervous anxiety he always felt when he was to speak in public usually took away his appetite, — and was on his way to Bowman's Hill, as the keeper of the "Cosmopolitan Hotel" informed him they had christened the bluff at the northern end of the town. As he turned in the street, and looked back at what in his Eastern home would have been popularly called a "tarvern," he smiled at the ludicrous suggestion, that, if the name had been any bigger for so little a hotel, the signboard would have stuck out at both ends of the building. And the term "Cosmopolitan" had in it painful suggestions of the boundless hospitality the house afforded to all the inferior forms of animate life.

But he soon forgot the unpleasant breaks in his "visions of the night," as he thought that "God made the *country*, but man made the town." The scene of beauty about him was, at any rate, God's work, whatever might be said of the hotel. He slowly climbed the hill; for as he was to speak, not read, that day, he wisely thought a breath of the divine inspiration of nature would be fitting preparation.

When he had gained the hill, he looked slowly round, and drank in the scene. As he gazed down and up the river, and over the prairie beyond, and saw the city so silent at his feet, while the still sunlight, like magic alchemist, transmuted every base thing, even the filthy streets, to burnished gold, his lips moved, and his thoughts found involuntary utterance in those words that have become a part of so many fair nature-pictures, —

> "Oh, what is so rare as a day in June?
> Then if ever come perfect days."

And glancing up at the tender blue that seemed so near, and then away to where it softly rested on the as tender green of the prairie, he continued, —

> "Then heaven tries the earth, if it be in tune,
> And over it softly her warm ear lays, —
> Whether we look, or whether we listen,
> We hear life murmur, or see it glisten."

And he exclaimed in sincere and simple devoutness, "O Lord, how manifold are thy works! in wisdom hast thou made them all."

His musing was interrupted by a rough voice that exclaimed, —

"Waal, young man, I reckon as how ye must be fresh in these parts, or ye wouldn't be up here at this time in the mornin' alone, gawkin' round ez ef ye'd never seen a river nur a payrarie before."

Mark turned, and faced a man bare-headed and in his shirt-sleeves, who appeared to belong to an odd-looking and

diminutive cottage not far away. When he saw he was good-
natured, and disposed to be neighborly, he was not altogether sorry to be interrupted in his meditations; for he
thought he could ask him a few questions about the city
below. So he answered pleasantly, —

"Yes: I presume I am one that you'd call 'fresh,' having
come to town for the first time by last night's boat; and I
never saw the Mississippi till yesterday."

"Raally!" said he, "that seems sorter strange to one who's
looked at it night and mornin' for nigh thirty year. I reckon
it's natur' though. 'F I should go to Chicago or St. Louis,
I reckon I sh'd stare round same's you do here. Ye don't
look like a hotel-runner nur a book-agent?"

The tone of voice in which the last sentence was uttered
turned it into a question; and, as Mr. Forrest had no objection to his knowing his mission, he said,—

"No: I'm a minister. I preach my first sermon here to-
day. Perhaps you attend what is to be my church."

"Haven't been ter church this ten year," said he, "'cept
to funerals. I don't take much stock in what the churches
calls religion any more, nohow. I b'long ter the church o'
all-out-doors, where all the pews is free, and it don't cost
nothin' for choirs, coz the birds do the music. The churches is full o' ornery critters, that cheats week-days, and prays
Sundays. Now, thar's the Congregational church been
raarin' up a mighty fine meetin'-'us, but ain't got religion
enough ter go half way round. Presbyterians 'bout the
same, only their heaven's a leetle smaller'n the Congrega-
tionalists'. The 'Piscopals runs the Church of the 'Postolic

Succession, where they have sech 'a gentlemanly mode of worship,' as one on 'em said t'other day. 'N' then, wuss'n all the rest, is the Christ-yuns and Baptists, always fightin' 'bout a leetle more or less water, that wouldn't hurt 'em any outside, nur do 'em much good in. They talk so much 'bout water, that it always seems sort 'er swampy and soggy like, round a Baptist church, and makes ye feel 'z ef 'twas a kindo' speritooal fever-'n'-ager country they live in."

"Oh! but you're rather hard on the churches, aren't you?" said Mr. Forrest. "I know they're not all saints; but that is because they don't live out the beauty of their religion. It's more religion, not less, that we all need."

"Maybe, young man," said he; "but you'll be wiser when ye git older. Ask yer parding for speakin' rough; but I like yer, and am sorry ye ain't doing something better'n preachin.' Now, they had a feller here not long sence, that looked so ornery 't I thought the Lord must be short on't fer hands when he made a 'postle er him. But you look like a squar' man, az ef yer hed it in yer."

"Thank you for your good opinion," answered Mark. "Perhaps you'll think better of my religion when you know its better side."

"Ez ter that," said he, "I don't own up ter bein' 'thout religion now: only I've got my own kind. I've my own notions 'bout God an' this ere universe. I don't believe that bluff over yander wuz made in six days. An' I think th' Almighty knew what he was 'bout from the fust. I 'low it don't stan' ter reason, that after he'd got things done, and called 'em 'good,' he found himself dis'pinted in the way the machine run, and had ter come in an' fix 't all over again, and lose the biggest part o' the job at that. 'Cordin' ter you ministers, the Lord gits euchred every time, coz the other feller holds all the trumps."

"Well," said Mark, "I haven't time to talk longer now. I've heard you through, and some day I'll give you my side of these questions. I must be getting ready for church. Good day — what may I call you?"

"Call me Uncle Zeke, if you will. That's my every-day name. I live over thar' in the cabin. Latch-string's allers out."

Mr. Forrest now started down the hill, and walked leisurely in the direction of the church. He was not at all troubled by what he tolerantly regarded as the natural prejudices of one who had doubtless received rather ill usage at the hands of the world.

As he went on, he saw Major Ward, the gentleman who had met him East, and who drove him to his hotel. He had now come to walk with him to the church. Mr. Forrest related his adventure ; and the major gave him some account of Uncle Zeke, whom he spoke of as a "good, honest man, but a little peculiar."

The bells were now ringing out on the soft, luminous air ; and the streets were full of people on their way to church. Seeing Mr. Forrest with the major, they knew he must be the new minister, and so scanned him curiously as they passed.

"The people are taking my measure, major," said he. "They are looking to see if I am a 'reed shaken by the wind.'"

"It'll be an old story after a little, and I think you'll enjoy
it when you get settled into the work. This is a field of
most capital promise."

They had now reached the church, a plain but nice brick
structure, on the corner of Seventh and Linden Streets,
facing the public square. Mr. Forrest saw, through the open
door, that it was filled by a pleasant and attractive-looking
congregation. He passed up the aisle, and took his seat in
the pulpit. He was used to facing congregations by this
time ; and so, while modest in demeanor, he was not flurried.
For the first time in his life, however, he *was* afraid of eyes ;
not of the hundreds, but of one solitary pair. These —
the eyes of the angel that floated into his yesterday's vision
— looked at him, and pierced him through and through.
He trembled, and looked down. To him this large audience
was now reduced to one. He wished she might have staid
at home on this first Sunday, until he had once been heard.
He did not care whether the people liked the sermon :
would *she* like it? It was not a sense of pride in his work,
but only the crushing thought that he could not bear to have
her hold a mean opinion of him. The sweetest flowers
would have shrivelled to a poor and unworthy gift, if he had
thought of offering them to her. And so his highest and
best thoughts seemed poor, because she was to listen.
Would she think him awkward? This thought almost paralyzed his movements.

But the time came to speak ; and he bravely flung away
his timidity, and began the service.

He took for his text, " God was in Christ, reconciling the

world unto himself.". He preached a sermon of nature and of life. The sweet world and the blue sky, and the high hope of a young and noble heart, got into his words. He spoke of God as the living and loving God to-day ; of Christ as a manifestation of his saving grace that waited not to be sent for, but went out after the lost ; of man as able to turn from evil when he would ; and he closed by saying, that, if any men were finally lost, it would only be because they " would not come and have life."

At the close of service he had what to him was the exquisite pleasure of touching Miss Margaret's hand once more. And, though she said no word of the sermon, there was that in her eyes that told him she had been melted and moved. And he went out of church as light as air, feeling that all the world might hate and despise him, if it would, provided only her eyes might look upon him with approval.

After being introduced to everybody, he accepted an invitation to dine with Major Ward. And we will leave him now in his care, while we listen to a few comments in the vestibule and on the street.

"Oh ! that was a sweet, gentle, loving sermon, wasn't it ? " said old Mr. Buck.

"Yis," said aunt Sally Rawson ; "but I don't think he'll never do. He'll be too foppish, I'm afeared : his hair curls too much for a minister."

"And there's another thing," said old Mrs. Buck : "he'd orter be married. A minister ain't wuth nothin' till he's got a wife to help him do his parish work. An' I guess there won't be much spiritooality about him as long's he's gallivantin' round with all the handsome gals. Now, my old man was nothin' till I took him in hand, and settled him down; and he ain't a minister neither."

"Oh, yes!" tartly replied Jane Ann Rawson, "of course you'll talk that way, because you ain't got any girls. If you had one fit to be married, you'd think he was a special providence."

And so the chatter ran on. The quiet ones went away and thought. The rattlers went away, and rattled as they went. But they meant no harm by their gossip, and were as ready to like the new minister as anybody.

The only thing that boded trouble was the comments of three that went up the street by themselves, — Judge Hartley, Mr. Richard Smiley, and Deacon Putney, who, on account of his plastic nature, was generally called Deacon Putty by any one who was speaking of, and not to, him. If you wanted to know his opinion, you must hunt up the last strong-minded man who had spoken to him. He meant well: so of all stupid tools and blunderers. Meaning to serve the Lord, he was always ready to do the Devil's work, if his highness only came playing his popular part of the "angel of light."

"I like him capitally," said Deacon Putney: "that was just a splendid sermon."

"Well," replied Judge Hartley, "I'm afraid it savors a little too much of tenderness towards sin. Of course God is love; but he's justice too. The wickedness of man needs the wrath preached. God is love toward the elect; but to the hardened sinner he is a 'consuming fire.' But I won't

judge too soon : he may give us the other side next Sunday."

"And I think," said Mr. Richard Smiley, "that such
preaching is fast verging toward infidelity. Not a word
about 'justification by faith ; ' not a word about the 'rags
of our own righteousness ; ' not a word about total depravity, and the uselessness of a man's trying to help himself
and lead a good life in his own strength ! I believe that
the 'works of the law' are a curse, and that what we need
is 'free grace' through the blood of Christ."

He didn't know enough of the true meaning of scripture to understand that it was just the "works of the law,"
in Paul's sense of the term, to which he was really trusting.
And Uncle Zeke on the bluff sometimes shrewdly observed,
that, if "Dick Smiley ever is saved, it will have to be by
faith, sure 'nough. For, d'ye see, he hain't got rags o' self-
righteousness 'nough round his whole place to rig out a
'spectable scarecrow."

But Deacon Putney, after the *ex-cathedra* opinion of Mr.
Smiley, made nimble work of getting over the critical fence ;
and said, —

"Well, yes : I guess p'raps there's a deal in what you say.
We'll have to keep our eyes open, and see that he don't win
the affections of the church, and lead 'em into infidelity."

Meantime, at the house of Major Ward, Mr. Forrest was
finding pleasant and appreciative entertainment. The major
wholly approved of the sermon, and gave him a hearty right
hand on the promise of his first Sunday in Bluffton.

V.

TO THE CAVE.

MR. FORREST had now been several weeks at Bluffton, and was quietly settled down to his work. The other two of the judge's daughters had come on from Chicago, and the family was established in its new home. Mr. Forrest had wearied of the hotel, and been admitted into the house of a family close by the judge's, and had fitted up the "best room" as his study. The people had exhausted their petty criticisms, and, when they were done, found out that they really liked him amazingly. So thoroughly had he gained the ear and respect of the town by his straight-out, simple manliness, that even Mr. Richard's Smiley's instinctive dislike was hidden beneath a cloak of seeming admiration. And of course Deacon Putney was loud in his praises. Judge Hartley, who, where he did not consider the honor of God or the integrity of the gospel at stake, was as gentle and loving as a child, had been thoroughly won over into a genuine admirer of Mr. Forrest, and tried to make him feel that his house was a sort of home. He was at liberty to come and go as he would ; and always there was a chair for him at the table. And yet there was no house

where he felt less free.   Perfectly well-bred, and accustomed
to pass at ease through all phases and forms of society, —
having the perfect assurance and self-control which always
seems to fascinate women, who, weak themselves, instinctively admire the strong, — he yet felt in Madge's presence a
certain awe and constraint such as a Catholic might feel in
approaching the shrine of a saint.

So much at home did he at length become in the family,
that they talked, read, walked, and rode together.   He could
not decline these common courtesies without appearing to
be unaccountably odd : he did not wish to decline them, for
he was irresistibly drawn to her side.   And yet he could not
conceal from himself the fact that he was risking the peace
and happiness of his life.   She had become a part of his
waking and sleeping thoughts.   He could not bear to think
of the future with her face and form left out ; and still he was
compelled to confess that he had no reason to suppose he
could win her.   And indeed it seemed like infinite presumption to think of calling her his own.   All first, true love is
worship ; and it seems like profanation for a mortal to expect any thing more than a smile, or permission to kiss her
hand, from the goddess he adores.   The ground she trod on
was holy.   If her dress accidentally brushed him in passing,
it thrilled him through and through as young trees thrill at
the touch of the spring-time sun.   The commonest article
of apparel that she had worn was consecrated, and fit to
become a sacred relic.

The house where he boarded was just across the street ;
and her chamber was opposite and facing his.   As the

Parsee salutes the rising sun, and then goes to his labor, so he felt stronger for his daily task if, in her fresh morning wrapper, she bestowed upon him a smile and a nod as she threw open her window to breathe the sweet summer air, and sprinkle the thirsty flowers and vines that turned the window-seat into a sort of hanging garden. And sometimes he would sit by his window, and read his own thoughts and longings in the dainty verse of Aldrich : —

" With lash on cheek she comes and goes;
   I watch her when she little knows:
      I wonder if she dreams of it.
   Sitting and working at my rhymes,
   I weave into my verse at times
      Her sunny hair, or gleams of it.

Upon her window-ledge is set
A box of flowering mignonnette :
   Morning and eve she tends to them, —
The careless flowers that do not care
About that loosened strand of hair,
   As prettily she bends to them.

If I could once contrive to get
Into that box of mignonnette,
   Some morning when she tends to them —
She comes ! I see the rich blood rise
From throat to cheek ! — down go the eyes
   Demurely as she bends to them."

He would have given the world to know that she would care to have him as near to her as the mignonnette. Then he would torture himself with deliberately making up his mind that of course she cared nothing for him, and never would. "She," he would think to himself, "is a native-born princess. Some rich man will come, and fill her hair with jewels, and spread soft, deep carpets for her dainty feet, and make her at home in rooms full of pictures and the art-treasures of the world. I am only a poor minister. What can I offer her? A parsonage and parish work; and take her into the midst of a set of meddling, criticising fools, who think the minister's affairs are public property, who will find fault with every rose she wears in her hair, and will think her merry laughter is sinful levity in a minister's wife. Bah! it would be an insult to ask her to do it, and she is too proud and wise ever to consent. By as much as I love and worship her image, —

> 'I must tear it from my bosom,
> Though my heart be at the root.'"

And then he would plunge into his study, or rush out and dive into his parish work, or wander off for a walk upon the hills.

Three or four miles down the river was a cave, — a sort of Mammoth Cave on a smaller scale. It was full of chambers, and passage-ways, and natural wonders. As, then, it was always of interest in itself, and as there was a fine open grassy glade in front of its mouth, where grand old trees gave abundance of pleasant shade, and through whose branches was a lovely view of the river, it was a favorite resort for picnic and pleasure parties. To the cave, therefore, the young people had now arranged an excursion; and of course they invited the minister to accompany them. They had engaged the little steamer, the Eagle Wing, to carry the party. But Mr. Forrest had discovered that Miss Margaret — as near familiarity as he could persuade himself to approach in addressing her — was extravagantly fond of horseback riding; and, as this was one of his California accomplishments, he determined to offer her the pleasure of a gallop. Thinking she might shrink from going with him alone, he invited one of her sisters and a gentleman friend to make up their equestrian party of four.

They started an hour before the merry steamer-load; and, taking a circuitous and unfamiliar road, they determined to enjoy a leisurely 'lope, and, coming in to the river below the cave, be on hand to meet the party on the boat as they landed. It was a wild, merry ride. Mr. Forrest often said that he knew of nothing like the sense of thrilling, exulting, godlike power that one experiences mounted on a nervous but well-trained horse, so adapted to his rider that they become one like the half-divine centaurs of old. The only thing that ever reminded him of it was the similar sense of mastery that he sometimes experienced when preaching at his best, with no fence of a desk between him and his audience; and when he was grasping in his hands, like reins, the invisible threads of sympathy that ran to every heart, and gave him power to sway, to rouse, to soothe, to make smile or weep, at will, — the exercise of a power that only the orator knows. So on they galloped through shade and sun; Mr. Forrest and Miss Hartley being mounted on a pair of splendid grays. They chatted merrily as they walked their horses up some rising ground, or stopped to breathe them for a moment in

the shade. It was a pretty picture of health and vigor and
beauty : their light and happy laughter ringing out on the
fresh morning air ; their young blood keeping time to the
rhythmic motion, mounting to the red cheek, and giving
the eye an added lustre ; the while they sped onward through
the checkered sunlight beneath the trees, plunged through a
shady thicket, leaped some narrow stream, and then shot
out into the gleaming sunshine again ; themselves a part of
the old world's everlasting youth.   The Tennysonian ride of
Queen Guinevere kept dancing through his brain ; and, could
he but be her Launcelot, he felt he could ride the world forever, if she would but lead, and make him rich in payment
of her smile.   They were surprised at every turn by pictures
of beauty, that, but for the more thrilling fascination of simple motion, they would have liked to stop and enjoy.   But
when they gained the highest point of their ride, as they
turned toward the river, such a panorama spread around
them that they all, as if by common consent, reined in their
horses.   For thirty miles the magnificent river wound, gleaming and sparkling, in full view.   It was a stream of silver,
gemmed with islands of perfect green.   Ten miles up stream
curled the smoke of a steamer, too far away to be any thing
but a silent part of the picture.   Ten miles down stream,
climbing up on to and crowning the top of a bluff, gleamed
the white and shone the red of a city, while a light cloud
of smoke hung over it in the still air.   Across the river, the
prairie, farms, farmhouses, villages, a train of cars shooting
across the green, and a low range of hills that cut off the
view.   Behind them a wondrously diversified country, of hill

and vale, made picturesque by strips of red country road and the varied shade of green or brown of the different crops of corn or grain or grass.

"Never was any thing fairer than this seen since Moses stood on Pisgah!" exclaimed Mr. Forrest.

"I don't see how heaven can be any finer," said Miss Hartley.

They were too full of the wondrous beauty of the scene for common conversation. As they sat and simply gazed, Mr. Forrest glanced at his watch, and said; —

"It's almost time for the boat: we must hurry on."

They spurred their now rested horses in a merry race, and soon stood on the river road that ran along close by the bank. They found themselves about a quarter of a mile below the cave; and the Eagle Wing was in sight. But she was getting on after a fashion that Mr. Forrest had never seen before. He was too keen an observer to pass by any important thing without learning its use: so he had already discovered that the two spars, attached to either side of the upright pole on the bow of a river-boat, were used for "creeping" over sand-bars.

"Hallo!" called out Mr. Snyder, the knight of Miss Margaret's sister Sue, "the Eagle Wing doesn't fly very well to-day, does she?"

And, as they could do nothing but look on, they trotted leisurely along to get a better view of the situation.

"I'd no idea the river was so shallow," said Mr. Forrest.

"It's deep enough," returned Mr. Snyder, "if one can only keep the channel. But during the high water, and when the current is rapid, the bottom shifts so that it is hard for even the best pilots to keep the run of it. Then, as the water falls rapidly, no one knows when he may get aground. So, you see, they always go prepared for a ' creep.' "

" See her lift," said Miss Margaret. " It must be a queer sensation to sail on stilts in that style."

The little steamer was doing bravely. The two long spars, fastened together at the top of the upright pole, were thrust out forward and on either side, forming a sort of letter A without the cross-stroke. Then, as they put on all steam, the spars acted as a lever to raise the bottom from the sand ; and she sprang forward until the spars pointed toward the stern, and she was resting on the bar again. As her load was light, and the bar was not a very extensive one, a few lifts like this took her over into free water again. The party on the boat set up a shout, which was answered from the shore ; and in a few minutes the planks were out, and the happy crowd were scattered under the trees, and making ready to explore the cave.

With bits of tallow-candles for torches, and strips of news-paper for candlesticks, they threaded the narrow passage-ways, passed through lofty chambers, or stood on the edge of abysses, and listened to the drip of unseen waters that tum-bled down the dark ways of the eternal night below. Some of the chambers they illuminated with red and purple and yellow lights. One was like a cathedral with fretted roof, and pillared by the meeting and joining-together of stalac-tite and stalagmite. They tried to fling a ray down into St. Ronan's Well, a circular deep, to which no bottom had ever been discovered. A rock flung down passed into utter silence, and, when it struck, gave up no sound.

When tired of the cave, they had games and walks and talks, and then the lunch spread under the trees; and so the day flew on. Who ever knew a day to be long when measured off by the laughter and song and play and conversation of young men and women, with a grassy carpet beneath their feet, and a bright sun and a blue sky over their heads?

At last the party had re-embarked, and the riders were re-mounted. Instead of returning the way they came, they determined, for the sake of variety, to go home by the river road; and the playful project entered their heads, of letting the Eagle Wing get thoroughly under way, and then trying a race with her for the town. So, taking position, Mr. Forrest waved his hat in air, was answered by fluttering handkerchiefs from the steamer, and on they flew. For some distance they kept what would have been "neck and neck," supposing the steamer had had a neck; and then the horses got excited. The grays being the faster of the four, Mr. Forrest and Miss Hartley soon left their companions out of sight round a curve in the road. The wind fairly whistled by them, as it does through the rigging of a ship at sea. But, so long as the horses seemed happy, their riders cared not how fast they sped. Mr. Snyder and Sue Hartley, having given up the chase as useless, had reined in their horses, and were coming on by an easy lope, but still out of sight on the winding road. Mr. Forrest and Miss Margaret still sped on; when, suddenly turning a sharp curve in the road,

her horse caught the quick gleam of a white bowlder that
sprang into view so quickly, through the half-hiding trees,
that he had not time to see what it was. He reared and
plunged for a moment ; but so firmly and naturally did she
ride, that she seemed in no danger of being unseated. But
the fright had maddened him ; and now he plunged forward
so like the wind that even Mr. Forrest could not keep up.
She tried to rein him in, but he took the bit in his teeth ;
and as he turned another curve, and shot out of sight under
the trees, Mr. Forrest saw, with a horror that almost stopped
the beating of his heart, that one rein was broken, and she
could control him no longer. He spurred his own horse to
the utmost, and rushed on in pursuit. What next he saw
almost paralyzed him. The horse was out of sight ; and the
whole universe to him was now only that one white, still face
beside the road. " O God ! " he cried, " she is dead, and I
have killed her ! " His head whirled, and the light of
heaven seemed to go out in awful night, as he not dis-
mounted, but flung himself from his horse. What he did he
hardly knew, till he found himself some distance away, sitting on the grass by a little spring that trickled out of the
side of the hill, with her head on his knee, and bathing her
face with the cold water. An hour before, he would have
thought it presumption to dream of her being his : now his
heart leaped up and claimed her, and rebelled at fate for
thus perilling his title. He felt that she was his own, and
that some horrible power was snatching her away. Was she
dead? There was a slight bruise on her temple. She did
not seem to breathe. He chafed her hands, and felt for her

pulse, which was only a feeble and irregular flutter. He called to her, "Madge! Madge!" in passionate familiarity, for love and grief made formality a mockery: "would God I had died for you, or with you!"

The trees on the bank at this point shut out the steamer from view; and the party on board had not seen the accident. He tenderly laid her head upon his coat, which he stripped off for a pillow, and rushed into the road to see if her sister and friend were in sight. They were evidently taking the ride leisurely, and were nowhere to be seen. He rushed back, and again took her head upon his knee. He passionately kissed her forehead, and called to her again to see if his voice would wake her.

The tears fairly started for joy, as she now moved slightly, and a half-sigh escaped her. Her eyes opened just a little, and then closed again. Her lips moved as if they would speak; but were silent. He watched her breathlessly, with a joy and anxiety that did not seek for utterance. At last a murmuring came from her lips, that out of inarticulate nothings shaped broken fragments of speech, —

"Mr. For-rest! Mark! Save me!"

"Yes, Madge! dear Madge! I'd die to save you. Can you hear me?"

But she was still again. The blood now began to mount to her cheeks; and, as he watched her, he uttered his thought aloud: —

"Oh, what a lovely face!"

Just then she roused a little, and, having half-consciously caught the last words, said, in a dazed sort of way, —

"Who spoke of love?"

And then she blushed deeply, as she suddenly became conscious of where she was, and what she had said.

Mark saw that she had half caught his secret from those dimly-divined words; and hardly knew whether to be glad or sorry to have her guess the truth thus early. But it was now no time for any thing but gladness to see her wake, and hear her speak again.

As she roused, and recovered from her faint, the old awe with which he regarded her came back: she seemed to slip from his hands, and the gulf was between them again.

"Thank God, Miss Hartley, it is no worse!" he exclaimed.

At this point, her sister and Mr. Snyder appeared. A few words explained all. Astonished that no bones were broken, and that she had so soon recovered from the fainting-fit into which fear as much as the fall had thrown her, they found, on examination, that a clump of bushes had broken the force of her fall, and still contained fragments of her dress. Beside these bushes Mr. Forrest had found her, but he was too anxious at the time to notice it. A carriage was now procured from a neighboring farmhouse; and, while she leaned upon her sister, Mr. Forrest drove them home. Mr. Snyder, riding his own horse, led the other two, and found the fourth in his stall.

When arrived at Mr. Hartley's house, Mr. Forrest was obliged to take the still weak Miss Margaret in his arms, and half carry, half assist her to her chamber. He then hastened for a physician; and, learning that probably there was nothing more serious than a nervous shock that would confine her to her room and lounge for a few days, he left, with many expressions of self-blame for her fall, and of wishes for a night of quiet sleep.

VI.

THE CONVALESCENCE.

MR. FORREST slept little that night; for his brain ran on like a music-box wound up, with the case fastened, and of which he had lost the key. The tunes it played were beyond his control. It wailed or danced, sang hope or despair, apparently according to its own mood. And, when it did lull enough to let him sleep, it appeared to whirl on still in dreams. He rode wild horses, and was flung down bottomless abysses. The face of Miss Hartley was by his side, he held her hand, and was about to tell her his love, when suddenly the figure would fade away, and he would find himself alone in some wild place, listening to voices of mocking laughter. Again, she was dead, and he, as minister, was tortured with the thought that he must attend her funeral, while no one knew that it was his right to sit broken-hearted as chief mourner. Or it was a wedding scene in church, where she was bride and he the happy groom; and then suddenly it was some one else that held her hand, and he was the minister, in hopeless agony, reading the marriage-service that was separating her from him forever.

But all mornings break at last, and so did this. As early as he thought propriety permitted, he went over to call upon her. He was shown up to her room, and found her in morning wrapper, upon her lounge, half sunk in easy pillows. She was suffering no pain, and was only weak and pale. But her sickness so became her, that he thought she never looked so beautiful. Her dark masses of loosened hair so framed the round, fair face and the lustrous eyes, and mouth that was a Cupid's bow, that he wished he were a painter, that he might keep the picture forever.

"Good-morning, Miss Margaret," said he. "I hope the results of my yesterday's mischief are not serious."

"Oh, no!" she replied. "I feel quite well, only they will make me lie still."

"Did you sleep?"

"Very well indeed. I always do. A good conscience, you know," she added with a playful smile.

"No trouble with your conscience in this instance: it is my conscience that is now at fault. The whipping furies have lashed me severely for putting you in such peril."

"Why, it was no fault of yours. I had a glorious ride, and I'd try it again: only I think I *would* see if the bridle was strong."

"You're a brave girl," said he; "and I am happier than I can tell you, to find you so well, and to learn that you do not blame me. I shall blame myself, however, just the same. And now, to prove that you forgive me, you must grant me permission to help assist in your cure."

"That, perhaps, will depend upon your medicine."

"Well, I know you are fond of reading, and yet you mustn't read to-day. The hours will be long, if you do nothing. May I read to you a while?"

"But isn't your parish work taking all your time?"

"Aren't you a part of my parish? And isn't my first duty to the sick?" said he, with a mock solemnity.

"Yes; but I've heard you say you didn't like parish work," said she archly.

"Well, then," said he laughing, "since you have such a good memory, I'll spend the day in reading to you 'from a sense of duty,' or for any other mentionable motive whatsoever, only so you will let me have my way."

So it was arranged that he was to read. As he rose to go to his study for some books, she said, —

"If you are to be my servant to-day, will you promise to obey orders?"

"Any thing in the wide world," said he.

"Well, then, read what else you will, but I command you to bring along some of your own verses; for I've heard that you write."

"I did not think you would use your new-found power in tyranny like this so soon. Indeed, I never confessed to being a poet."

"But people don't always confess their sins in public. I know you write; and, if you wish my forgiveness for it, you must read me some of your verses."

"If I must, I must: I've a few little snatches. And, if you make the conditions of my sitting with you so hard, of course I must comply."

"I am inexorable," she said: "so you know your fate."

He said to himself, as he looked over his portfolio, —

"If I must read my own lines, I'll take my revenge by making her hear the echoes of my own heart, and see if I can thus make out her own. I'll invent a Hamlet plot, and see if her face confesses any care for me."

He soon returned. He read first from Tennyson's "Princess," and they talked over some of its many problems. Then they went over some of the sweeter "Idyls of the King," and discussed the virtues of knighthood and the old ideals of womankind. At last she said," Now let me hear your own."

"'Oh, what a fall was there, my countrymen!'" said he, laughing. "From Tennyson to Forrest, — the author only of several unpublished manuscripts. But I may as well be slaughtered now as to anticipate it longer."

He picked up some loose papers, and continued, —

"The first is a foolish little song. You know I only scratch off rhymes for recreation, and because my thoughts will sometimes jingle. I have entitled it

THE QUESTION.

'Oh! tell me how to woo and win,'
   The shepherd sang. The echoes flew
Adown the vale, now loud, now thin,
   And answered only, 'Win and woo!'

'But I am not a shepherd lad :
   So tell *me*, echo sweet,' said I,
'How shall *my* heart's long wish be had?'
   'Had — wish you had,' was its reply.

'No common word can make her mine ;
  No common love do I adore :
  Toward me does *her* heart incline ? '
  But echo would reply no more.

"No, Miss Margaret, " said he as soon as he finished : " I shall not wait, and make you struggle between courtesy and veracity ; but, without letting you rest, you must listen again. You've brought it on yourself, you know.

WILL LOVE DESCEND ?

A heaven-born goddess is sweet Love :
  Will she descend to common cares ?
  And breathe our dusty, earthly airs
In narrow paths, nor pine to rove ?

She'll want soft carpets for her feet ;
  She'll want rich jewels in her hair,
  From out her windows landscapes rare,
And in must float all perfumes sweet.

She'd weary of a petty round
  Of household tasks that every day
  Fritter and fret the life away, —
Though husband worshipped, children crowned.

Yes, heart that thought the heavens to scale,
  And pluck a star from her bright zone,
  Stars are too high to call thine own :
Go, seek a rushlight in the vale."

"Well, I can't let you go on any farther until I protest against that," said she. " It isn't a heaven-born goddess that looks upon life in that way. True love is always humble. I know nothing of men's hearts; but it seems to me, that, if a woman *should* love a man, she would always look up to him, and be exalted by her love, whatever his station might be. Stars that will not shine in vales are no true stars. And any man would be degraded who should stoop to what he would be compelled to think of as beneath him."

"You think a true woman, then, would marry a man without regard to his station?"

"Of course I think so."

"But isn't Tennyson's line too true? —

'Every door is barred with gold, and opens but to golden keys.'"

"I don't think it is, except with some who can appreciate nothing else. It isn't strange that a woman should like fine houses, horses, and money, any more than that a man should, I suppose."

"Certainly not. But what if a man, recognizing that, should hesitate to ask a woman's love because he lacks them?"

"Then he deserves to go without her love. If he has brains, or character, why not offer them? A true woman must despise a man who thinks she is in the market to be sold to the highest bidder. I know some women do sell themselves for homes; but so do men too, for that matter, when they hunt for rich wives. But what are those other verses?"

Mark felt that he had learned one thing, at least; and his minister's lot did not seem so poor as when he feared she might have higher worldly aspirations. So he read on, —

What shall one do with a hopeless love?
    If he bury it in his heart,
Too strong for its prison it will prove,
    And burst its walls apart.

If he bury it in the sea, 'twill arise
    When the evening love-star gleams,
And, mocking him with its deathless eyes,
    Will haunt him in his dreams.

If he bury himself in his books, and seek
    To hide him from its sight,
'Twill laugh at his Hebrew and his Greek,
    And mock him as in spite.

If he do not seek its face to flee,
    And yet no hope is given,
'Twill make of life a misery,
    And make a hell of heaven.

"We won't say any thing about that," said he : "it helps
pass the time.   But here is the last.   I have named it, —

THE CRIME AGAINST LOVE.

Love was a judge, and he held a court
    With the culprit in the box.
He had flung him into his jail, — Despair, —
    Close under double locks.

The crier cried, and the court began.
    The attorney rose and said, —
'The prisoner at the bar, my lord,
    We charge, as shall be read.'

And he read a long indictment through,
    That charged contempt of love.
'He has spoken slightingly of you,
    As I'll proceed to prove.

'He has said, "I'll travel other lands;
    I'll wed my books and lore:
Divine philosophy alone
    Shall my fond heart adore.

'"Love is the passion of weak minds:
    I will not be its slave.
Love is a blindness of the eyes,
    And it is reason's grave."'

The indictment through, the attorney said,—
    'My lord,—whom heaven defend!—
If words like these unpunished go,
    Your kingdom's at an end.'

'Speak, prisoner!' then the stern judge cried,
    'If you have aught to say.'
'I did not know you, mighty Love:
    I therefore pardon pray,—

'If ignorance may be excuse.'
    'Then hear me,' Love replied.
'Go seek the loveliest one you know,
    And by her word abide.

'If *she* forgives you, then will I:
    You have six months' release.'
And now he wanders up and down,
    And nowhere findeth peace.

He's seen the loveliest; but in vain!
   He cannot bring his heart
To risk the trial, lest he die
   If she should say, '*Depart!*'"

"Well," said Miss Margaret, "that is very prettily told. If you can write like that, you'll give the world a volume of verse some day. But I don't think the *culprit* is specially brave; do you?"

Mark was about to reply; and perhaps might have owned to being the culprit himself, had not the reading been suddenly cut short by the calling of some friends who had been on the excursion the preceding day. Having learned of the accident, they had come to see how seriously she was hurt.

She thanked him heartily for his kindness, and asked him to read again; then, taking his papers and books, he hurriedly withdrew.

VII.

OTHER STRANDS IN THE THREAD.

AND now we must take note of other strands that were being woven into the thread of Mr. Forrest's destiny. Life is not all love; and those things that seem farthest removed from its tender pleasure and its tender pain are so intimately wound up with it in human experience, that we cannot understand either strand when taken by itself. As one could not comprehend the turbid tide of the Mississippi, below its junction with the Missouri, unless he knew that two different rivers had become one, so the turbid, mingling, dividing, darkening, brightening current of Mr. Forrest's onward career can only be understood as we take note how the one stream of his life is henceforth compounded of love not only, but also of hope and fear, of inclination and duty, of old tradition and new thought,— all in relentless struggle. The sphinx's riddle had been given him to answer; and he felt that he must answer it, to the satisfaction at least of his own soul, or conscience, manhood, and self-respect would die. And, even if he could have won Miss Hartley with a lie in his hand, he would have felt he was offering her a hollow, rotten-hearted sham, and not the oak-hearted manhood that she deserved.

So all the time since he had been in Bluffton, he had been fighting a battle, that, to his thought, meant life or death. Several times he had been on the point of offering Miss Hartley his hand; and then had shrunk back, deterred by the thought that he had no right to do it until she fully knew all that was in his head as well as what was in his heart.

To find what this was that was in his head, — the elements of his great conflict,— we must go back, and take a brief glance at the more immediate past.

It has been already intimated, that, even in the theological seminary, Mr. Forrest admitted into his thinking a principle fatal to his "soundness." He had asserted the ultimate principle of Protestantism, "the right of private" individual "judgment;" and this, not only in interpreting the standards of the faith, but even as to the solidity of the foundations on which rested the faith itself. It is easy enough for an unprejudiced outsider to see that the Protestant principle, "the right of private judgment," leads logically to rationalism. For he who assumes to question the basis of authority, in that very act becomes a rationalist; that is, asserts the supreme right of reason to pass upon these ultimate problems; and that is what rationalism means. But, like many a young man who launches his craft on this Protestant sea, and feels in his sails the fresh and inspiring impulse of this Protestant free air, he had little thought out over what wide and pathless oceans, and under what threatening skies, he would drift before he rested again in any quiet harbor.

In his California life, he had found himself in a free and bracing air. Men there cared more for practical religion than for theoretical details of thought. And though he made himself, so far as he could, familiar with the best modern thought on scientific and critical subjects, he was still so busy in practical affairs, that he did not often stop to think whether there was place in his old theology for his new ideas. The gospel of the Christian life was what he cared for; and if now and then the critical question came up as to whether the system of his old faith could stand the strain of his newer knowledge, he allowed himself to be easily satisfied with the never-failing new exegesis that never hesitated in its attempt to reconcile the most seemingly hostile opposites. So he entered on his work in Bluffton, supposing himself orthodox, so far as he had given it any attention.

He had been there but a little while, however, before the subject loomed up on his mental horizon as a cloud that had lightning in it, and threatened storm. Several causes conduced to this; and now for a little it must be our business to trace them.

On coming to Bluffton, he had come into sharp, practical contact with the "five points of Calvinism" embodied in the unsympathetic, unyielding angularities of real people. The shock of this contact waked him up to the consciousness that that was not the kind of religion he believed in. A man may go on for years supposing himself to be holding faithfully to a system of thought that he has inherited and learned to reverence, while all the time the play of study and experience about it has totally changed its structure, and he wakes up to find that the old has disappeared. Just as an iceberg starts out, blue and hard and angular, from its

northern birthplace among the glaciers : it floats majesti-
cally and threateningly on, appearing like its original self,
while all the time the warmer airs have played around it, the
warmer seas have rippled against its sides, and it has become
honeycombed through and through.   Now let it strike some
rock of reality, or encounter some ocean storm, and, like a
mirage, it is gone : the seas have swallowed it forever.

So Mr. Forrest was rudely roused to the thought that the
gospel he held and preached was not what was popularly
held as orthodox.   He did not welcome the thought, nor
yield it an easy victory.   All the drift of inheritance and
tradition was in the old channel.   His childhood's home
was an orthodox home.   The sacred memories of father, of
mother, of the old fireside circle, of household prayer and
song, of Sunday bells still chiming in memory over the old
fields, all seemed bitterly to reproach the new thoughts that
appeared to be traitor to the old.   Loved ones had died
looking forward to the orthodox heaven, and pleading with
him to meet them there,   Here were the associations and the
friends of his life.   Along this path lay the apparent way to
the attainment of all his earthly ambitions.   Dark shadows
also from the future seemed to threaten him.   He started
appalled sometimes at the thought, that, after all, these mis-
givings of his reason might be only the darkened wanderings
of a fallen nature.   The angel of darkness, robed as an
angel of light, might be thus playing with and tempting his
soul.   He would say, " Get thee behind me, Satan ! "

And then, on the other hand, he would reason, that, from
the beginning of the world, all who, like Abraham, like

Jesus himself, like Paul, like Luther, had left a past dear to sentiment and rich in precious memories, must have gone through substantially the same struggle of foreboding, of doubt, of misgiving. And, the more deeply he thought, the more he became convinced that this new light was not a will-o'-the wisp, leading him astray, but really the faint streaks of a new morning.

But now he would grow heart-sick at the thought, " Miss Margaret is thoroughly, fixedly orthodox in all her training and ways. The new light — if it *be* from heaven — will still lead me away from her." And this was to him bitterer agony than all the rest. He had hours when he felt like Adam in " Paradise Lost," when he found that Eve had eaten the apple. The outer wilderness with her would be dearer than paradise alone ; and he hardly knew if he would enter the open gate of heaven if it meant letting go her hand.

Another thing turned his thought into the same channel. He was talking with Judge Hartley one day, concerning the practical effects of religion on the life, when he ventured to remark, —

" There's one thing, judge, that troubles me immensely in my preaching. There are many people in the church not half so good as many that are out of it."

" So far as man can see, perhaps it may be so," cautiously answered the judge.

" And it seems almost hypocrisy in me to preach to those outside as sinners, and exhort them to repentance," he continued, " while the lightning ought to strike inside if any-where."

"But, Mr. Forrest, these outside fair livers are doubtless trusting to their own righteousness, which is a broken reed There is no evidence that they have the grace of God in their hearts."

"If these others had as much of the grace of God in their hearts as they pretend, wouldn't they have a little better character among men? What's the evidence of grace that doesn't show itself in works?"

"When one gets to talking too much of works, he is on dangerous ground," said the judge. "The curse of the law is on him who trusts in works."

"But isn't it a part of Christianity to have works?"

"Yes, morals are desirable, even necessary, in a true Christian. But they are worth nothing to a man who is not converted. They may even be a snare, a soul-destroying snare. If a man trusts in them, he is gone. Of course a man had better be sober than to be a drunkard; he had better be honest, and pay his debts, than to be a swindler; he had better be kind than cruel in his family. But, after all, Mr. Forrest, morals don't touch the question of salvation. The vilest sinner that trusts to the atoning blood is safer than the best man that ever lived, who comes into the presence of God in his own righteousness."

"Why, Judge Hartley," said Mr. Forrest, "that seems to me like putting a premium on immorality."

"Mr. Forrest," returned the judge, "however it seems to the carnal reason, it is the teaching of divine revelation; and I am astonished that a minister of the gospel should use such language."

"Well," he replied, " I may be all wrong: but upright living is better for *this* world than a religion that is consistent with dishonesty and uncharitableness; and, since the same God rules in the next world who governs this, it seems strange that the same principle shouldn't apply over there."

Mr. Forrest had been led on by his own thought, as he spoke, to the taking of a more advanced ground than he had foreseen when he began; and he found he had shocked the judge beyond measure. As they separated, the judge remarked, —

"Mr. Forrest, your first sermon troubled me just a little; not what you said, but what you didn't say. I feared you were not quite sound on some important doctrines. But you've been so manly and successful, that I'd been hoping the other side would be soon brought out with no uncertain sound. But you mustn't preach such thoughts as you've spoken to-day. You would make the whole gospel of no effect. What's the need of the cross, if such things are true?"

And the judge walked sadly away.

After this Mr. Forrest noticed that he watched him more narrowly as he preached, and that he was a little less cordial as they met. He found also, little by little, that he had let fall a word here and there, and that the more strictly doctrinal ones in the church were slightly changed in their manner toward him. He was still made formally welcome at his house; though now and then the judge made him remember their conversation, by advising him to a prayerful, humble study of the divine mystery of salvation by faith.

And one thing more was at this time moulding his present, and so shaping the future. When first roused to face the fact, that, for better or worse, his opinions were largely changed, he did not follow the denominationally safe method of rushing back out of the glare — whether of hell or heaven he knew not — that was blinding him, into the quiet shadows of the old traditions. Many is the man, in his case, who has refused to read what would "lead him astray." He has kept to denominational papers and reviews and books, and refused, by sheer force of will, to harbor unwelcome and unsettling thoughts. This seemed to Mr. Forrest the course of a sneak and a coward, and as such he despised it. But it also appeared to him downright dishonesty of thought. "We expect heathen and sceptics," he would say, "to drop all prejudice, and at least examine our claims. Then I'll at least be as brave. If I can't hold my religion in daylight, I'll fling it to the bats." So he began a course of systematic reading and study as to the foundations of his belief. He soon found that it was whispered about the parish, that he "actually had scientific and Unitarian books in his library;" and aunt Sally Rawson remarked at the sewing-circle, —

"What such things'll lead to, the Lord only knows."

Still he kept on studying and reading. He would have a "reason for the faith that was in him."

And he not only read and studied, but he went over with his friend Tom all the great questions of the age; and they tried to look at them before and behind.

As already intimated, he and his friend Tom Winthrop had been separated since they left college; and, while they had

kept up occasional friendly interchanges, neither of them
had taken the trouble to keep acquainted with the drift of
the other's thinking. Mark had known Tom — they were
still Mark and Tom to each other — as a somewhat fearless
and independent thinker, even in college; and as one inclined always to probe things to the bottom, to see what they
were made of. He was less emotional and enthusiastic than
Mark; and at times Mark was inclined to charge him with
being hard, and even inclined to a slight shade of cynicism,
in his conclusions. But still he was loving and generous;
and only anxious to know that either a thought or a man
was sound to the core, — no sham, — and he would stand
by them in good report or ill. He had a keen logical mind,
and — what is very rare in this world — a keen insight as to
the value of proof. For it is a strange fact that those men
— even educated men — are few who can weigh evidence
carefully, and so tell when a certain proposition is proved to
be true, and when it is not. Most men's minds are like ill-
constructed scales: they turn without much regard to the
weights.

With a mind like this, and with a well-prepared basis of
scholarship, Mark found that his friend had found time, during the years of their separation, to follow out his old lines
of study. Though busy as a man of business, he had still
pursued his private investigations. He had even written an
occasional article of local scientific importance, or had con-
tributed to some theological discussion in the reviews. Mark
found him well "up" in all the great questions of the day;
and that he not only had very positive opinions of his own,

but was quite prepared to do battle in their behalf. He was an out-and-out rationalist in his opinions concerning religion, though by no means bitter toward the training of his childhood. He had the tolerance of a wise believer in evolution toward the past; and would no more think of quarrelling with it than of whipping a boy for not being a man, or finding fault with the twilight because it wasn't noon. But, as he sometimes said, he had very little respect for a man who would keep his eyes shut tight at noon, and take his own stupidity for twilight. He felt like shaking such a man rather roughly, and telling him to open his eyes.

All these points, as to the mental condition of his friend, Mark gradually discovered as the months of his life in Bluffton had passed. They had renewed their old intimacy. Mark frequently took Monday for his rest-day, and would run up to Maple City, and pass it with Tom. And, when he could get leisure, Tom would come down and spend half a day with him. They would walk and talk together by the hour.

Mr. Forrest's association with his friend was a new point that gave the "straiter sect" in the church much trouble. Mr. Winthrop was a gentleman well known in Bluffton as a sharp, clear, and by no means orthodox thinker. Particularly was he obnoxious to Mr. Richard Smiley.

This Mr. Smiley, to whom we have already seen Deacon Putney so obsequious, was what Uncle Zeke called "the Great Mogul of the town." He employed the most men, and did the largest business. Though not superintendent, he had much to do with the Sunday school. Having an

oily tongue, and a good memory for anecdote, he capti-
vated the children. In a fifteen-minutes talk he would
have half of them in tears over the " dime-novel" style of
piety which he cultivated. He gave lavishly to the church
and public benevolent objects ; and the church bowed down
at his feet. As being able to bring the most tears, he was
the favorite speaker in prayer-meeting. He was the pet of
all the old women of the parish, because he would call, and
kneel down and pray and cry with them over " the state of
Zion." He had been a sore puzzle to the new minister ; for,
while stoutest in his defence of traditional orthodoxy, he
bore a most doubtful repute, as to his business-character,
among outside business-men. Even Deacon Putney one
day took Mr. Forrest aside, as they met on the sidewalk,
and said, —

" I tell you what it is : I don't know what to make of Mr.
Smiley. When you talk about his being a Christian, to the
best business-men down town, they think it's a good joke ;
and I've known of some things myself that weren't straight.
And yet, when he talks to me, blamed if he don't make me
believe he's a persecuted saint."

This was the man, then, that most strongly and loudly
objected to his minister's associating with " an infidel."
Mark did not know, at this time, what good reason Mr.
Smiley had for disliking Mr. Winthrop.

VIII.

MARK AND TOM TALK.

THE day on which Mr. Forrest had read with Miss
Hartley was Saturday. On Sunday he was very busy,
as usual, with his public duties; and on Monday it had
been arranged that Mr. Winthrop was to spend the day with
him. He had no time, then, to do more than call at the
door, send up his regards, and ask after Miss Hartley's
health. Finding that she was steadily improving, and was
likely to be out in a few days, he returned to his study,
wrote a few letters, and then went down to the levee to meet
his friend.

"Well, Tom, is it up at the study, or off for a walk on the
hills, this morning?" was Mark's first greeting as his friend
stepped off the plank.

"I think," replied Tom, "it would be almost wicked to
spend such a glorious Indian-summer day as this in the
house. Let's stretch our legs on the hills."

They leisurely climbed Bowman's Hill, and stood for a
moment to fill their lungs, and take in the wide beauty of
the scene.

"Tom," said Mark, "I've been over this country a good

deal; but, do you know, I've never seen weather so fine as the fall here in Bluffton: not even California excels it."

"Yes," replied Tom: "I do think it is unequalled. Just look over the river and the prairie yonder. The still air in the yellow sunlight is just liquid gold. And then it continues so, day after day, for weeks."

"Suppose," said Mark, "we take a run up the river, then strike inland and make the circuit of the hills, and come out on the bluff below the town. We haven't been up there yet together; and it is perhaps the finest view the city can boast."

So off they started. In a couple of hours they had made a round of six or eight miles, and stood on the crown of the great bluff. They now sat down to rest, and look about them. For a time they drank in the scene in silence. The city was at their feet; and it came so close to the foot of the bluff on one side, that they could have flung down a stone upon the roofs of the houses. On the river-side where they sat upon a knoll that formed a natural shelf, the bluff sank sheer down a hundred and fifty feet, to where the river rippled against the pebbles on the shore. A steamer was just passing; and they could almost have leaped upon its deck. Through the valley two or three miles away beyond the city, a train of cars was winding along like a serpent, and silently approaching the town. The little people, for such they looked from their high seats, were hurrying to and fro in the streets beneath, while Mark and Tom could easily imagine themselves like gods on Olympus, calmly overlooking the turmoil in which they had no part.

Here they sat, and fell into a long conversation, like many in which, during these times, they had been engaged.

"Mark, do you notice that long line of low bluffs about six miles away, across the prairie beyond the river, and running parallel with it north and south as far as we can see?"

"Yes."

"Well, that must be the old bank of the river, which ages ago filled this whole basin, and covered the place where all these farms and towns and railroads now are."

"Do you think so?"

"'Think' isn't the word: I know so. The waters have left the story of their own past work. The whole prairie yonder is a river-deposit; and the wave-marks are on the bluffs."

"How long ago do you reckon it was?"

"Oh! several thousand years. In geological time, ages are minutes; and a few more or less don't matter."

"You do not believe much in Moses, then, I suppose."

"Believe in Moses," said Tom: "why should I?"

"Why should you not? Couldn't God inspire a man to write a record of His work?"

"The question isn't whether he *could*, but whether he *did*; and that is a question of fact, to be settled on the evidence. Now Moses — or Genesis — says God created the world in six days, about six thousand years ago. And yet Niagara Falls are thundering in the ears of all the world, that will listen, the fact that it has taken at least two hundred thousand years for it to cut through a couple miles of rock from the present fall to the end of the rapids."

"But what of the new interpretation of Genesis, that makes the six days six periods of indefinite length?"

"Only a make-shift. The record says distinctly *days*, with evening and morning. And if the word 'day' doesn't mean day, how do you know what any other word means? And then the order of the world's growth does not agree with the Mosaic account, in spite of all the Procrustes stretching and clipping. And there is one principle I think it is safe to go by. Whether God wrote the Bible, or not, one thing we do know, the world is his work : nature is his book. What that says, then, is true, whether all the old-world guesses and dreams about it are true or not."

"But do you think that Moses wrote what he knew was not true?"

"Now, look here, Mark, that starts a large question. Let's go over the Bible a little, and see what we really know about it."

"At any rate, we know how long it has stood against all assaults, and how it has guided and comforted men."

"True enough so far : so have the Veda and the Tripitaka and Confucius and the Koran held their own; all but the last one, longer than the Bible. And they to-day comfort more people than all Christendom, several times over. We mustn't think we are everybody in the world."

"But at least the Bible is the book of civilization."

"Yes, because the races that have the Bible happen to be the ones that have in them the stuff to make a civilization out of."

"You do not think the Bible, then, the cause of civilization."

"Why should I, when its firmest adherents have fought advancing civilization at every step?"

"But that is the re-actionary spirit of Roman-Catholic conservatism."

"No, Mark, not at all. Protestantism in the churches has fought science as bitterly as Romanism. Luther was as severe against the knowledge that did not accord with his notions of revelation as ever the Pope was. Did you never read how he abused and ridiculed those who dared to think the world was round, and had inhabitants on the other side?"

"I had not noticed it."

"Well, what but that is the history of orthodoxy all through? It fights every thing new as long as it can. Then it re-interprets the Bible, and finds it all there, and benevolently takes it under the wing of revelation. It won't be ten years before a fast and firm alliance will be patched up between even Darwin and Moses. Moses will be made out the original Darwinian. Just so they treated Newton: they cursed his gravitation as long as they could; and now for two hundred years have been using the great law to glorify the Jewish conception of a God who taught a flat world 'founded on the seas and established on the floods.'"

"But is it not significant, that the Bible nations are the only ones to make progress?"

"First, it isn't true; and, next, if it were it would not be strange. The Bible didn't create religion: religions create Bibles. The highest, most moral, and most intellectual nations will produce the highest and purest sacred books;

just as the most intellectual nations produce the grandest epics, dramas, and works of art.

"But look here, Mark, let us look the Bible over, and see what claims it actually makes, and what its character really is. If there is any reason why we should always be fenced in with texts, all right : if not, then let us look over God's universe freely, and see things as they are, and not as people ages ago thought they were."

"Well," said Mark, "I have a thousand reasons for wishing to believe the Bible ; but I were a coward to shrink from investigating it. If it is God's book, it will bear looking at."

"What proof is there, then, that it is inspired?"

"Of course no intelligent man now holds the old theories of inspiration. Old Dr. Owen, you know, held that even the *Massoretic* points in the Hebrew must be inspired, or else we had no certainty as to its meaning. The verbal theories are now abandoned."

"But Dr. Owen was right," said Tom. "And, if it isn't verbal, it is all afloat. You say you only hold its essential teaching. But Christendom has never agreed as to what that is ; and now men, getting cornered on its scientific mistakes, say it is only inspired to teach morals. But its morals, even, are not always the best. So the cloud foundation shifts. Does the Bible claim to be inspired?"

"It says, 'All scripture is given by inspiration of God, and is profitable,' &c."

"Beg your pardon, but it doesn't," replied Tom. "Bishop Ellicott says the passage ought to read : 'All scripture, that is given by inspiration of God, is profitable,' &c. It doesn't say *what* scripture; and since, when that was written none of the New Testament was gathered, it couldn't refer to that, in any case."

"But the writers claim to have had divine guidance. Do you think they lied?"

"No: I think they were mistaken. The people of all the early ages supposed themselves to receive divine messages. They thought dreams and ecstasies, and all abnormal and mysterious manifestations of power and life, indicated super-natural presences and communications. I do not think any of the old religious founders and prophets, in any nation, were conscious impostors. They took for divine what we now know to be natural: that is all."

"But," said Mark, "how did a man living in Moses' time have such exalted ideas of God's nature and character, when all the rest of the world was in deep darkness? He must have been supernaturally illuminated."

"That starts just what I wanted to say. It is now settled conclusively, by modern criticism, that Moses was not the author of the Pentateuch, at all. In its present shape it is the product of the highest and latest thought of the Hebrew race. The grandeur of the first verse of Genesis represents the highest peak of Jewish civilization, and not the low starting-point. The Pentateuch is full of traces of a later age. It is just as if we should find in Shakspeare references to the telegraph and ocean-steamers. The five books are full of the finger-marks of the few centuries just preceding Christ. And then, what would be thought in a court of justice, of such proof as that on which men take the Old Testament?"

"Why, what do you mean?"

"I mean this: Nearly the whole Old Testament is anonymous. It is a national literature. Nobody knows who wrote
it, nor where nor when: only that we know it was *not* written — the most of it — in the way popularly supposed. It
is just a mass of traditions, national legends, and wonder-
stories, wrought into its present shape by unknown hands."

"But a moment ago you spoke disparagingly of its morals.
It is often urged as conclusive proof of its inspiration, that it
is a '*morally-winnowed*' book."

"'Morally-winnowed,' indeed! It isn't pleasant business
to pick flaws in the morals of the Bible; but it is safe to
say that the average tone of society to-day is infinitely
above the ordinary levels of the Old Testament. The character of Yahweh himself is such that he would not make
a respectable citizen of Bluffton to-day. Study it carefully,
and see. What of the morals of God's commanding the
Jews to capture and sack a city, to kill all the men, married
women, and children, and keep the virgins for the vilest pur-
poses?"

"Is that in the Old Testament?"

"You haven't read it carefully if you haven't found it.
What of the morals of polygamy and slavery? What of the
morals of supporting God's temple by bands of prostitutes,
as the Greeks did that of Venus? What of the morals of
the hundred and ninth Psalm? what of human sacrifices
practised clear down to the eighth century B. C.? what of a
cruel, jealous, revengeful God? Morals!" he exclaimed in
some excitement, "if a heathen nation were found practis-

ing Old-Testament morality, there would be new activity in the Bible Society to send them a new religion. These things are overlooked in the Bible, because a part of them are veiled in an obscure translation, and partly because people read with such a veil of superstitious reverence that they cannot see any defect in the idol they worship."

"But, whatever you think of the Old Testament, you must admit the divinity in the New."

"Well, let us see. Even some of the best orthodox critics — like Professor Smith of Aberdeen — admit that the Gospels are only 'non-apostolic digests' of earlier traditions. Such a man as Baring-Gould, orthodox and High-Church chaplain of the Queen, confesses that the New Testament is only 'the expression of the belief of the early Church.' No one knows who wrote either of the Gospels, except that it is pretty well known that John did not write the one attributed to him by after-tradition. Nearly the whole New Testament is anonymous, except the few genuine Epistles of Paul. And, even if it were not so, it only means that persons sixteen or seventeen hundred years ago believed so and so. I can't see why that is any reason why I should believe the same, apart from any evidence."

"But the morality of the New Testament" —

"Isn't absolute," broke in Tom, "any more than the Old. A man like Beecher confesses that it would overthrow society to put into wide practice the Sermon on the Mount. It is a beautiful ideal; but much of the best of modern civilization has come from *not* obeying it."

"What do you mean?" said Mark.

"Why, for instance, Christ forbids struggling for your rights, and commands non-resistance. Now, the whole progress of English liberty and the rights of man has come from disobeying it. It commands meekness and self-abnegation. All advance has come from self-development, and the Occidental spirit of daring, so opposed to the Oriental mysticism out of which the doctrines spring."

"Well," said Mark, "what else?"

"Not much more now, but only a word or two as illustration. Jesus teaches communism and against property. Civilization is based on the exact opposite of such teaching. It might be easy enough in the out-door life of Galilee to live like lilies and sparrows, 'taking no thought;' but it won't do here. And even there somebody had to work, and think, and plan ahead, or even the sparrows would have gone hungry.

"And then, Paul's morality is far from faultless. His doctrine of women is thoroughly degrading. They are only for the use of men, to keep those from being immoral who are not strong enough to lead a celibate life. He laid the foundation for all the monasticism of the middle ages."

"Well, Tom," said Mark, "you notice I've let you do all the talking; for I wanted to hear the utmost you would say. I've only asked questions enough to keep you moving. Don't think I can swallow it all."

"Don't swallow any of it until you are sure it is true," replied Tom.

"No," said Mark; "and when, if ever, I am convinced it is true, I will not shrink. Truth only is God; and truth must be followed, even if the Bible is lost."

"But you don't lose the Bible. Why will men talk in that way? You only find it: you find what it is. It isn't strange that it should have errors, and lower ideas of morals, if it is a human work. And then, the fact that so much of psalm and prophet and gospel and epistle is grand and noble and inspiring, gives the grandest promise for humanity, the moment you allow it to be a human work. The humanity that makes a Bible in its infancy, what may it not be in its fully-developed manhood?"

"But, Tom, it touches me more closely than you can think. It is every thing to me, — religion, my past life, my future prospects, and " — hesitating — " something I hardly dare think of."

"Why, what is it?"

"You remember your thoughtless remark about the judge's daughter, as we stood on the levee?"

"Yes; but what has she to do with this?"

"Every thing. I haven't spoke to you about it before, because I did not wish to confess my care for her until I had some reason to think she cared for me. I love her madly. I *think* she is not indifferent to me. But she would think me lost forever, did she know my religious thoughts, and guess the possibility of my becoming a heretic."

"Why don't you tell her, and see?"

"I'm a coward. I can't bear to think of paining her. And the judge would never consent. He'd think hell yawned beneath his daughter's feet."

"Are you engaged?"

"No; and I can't think it quite honest to ask her hand till she knows my doubts, and where my convictions may lead me."

"Well, Mark, old fellow," said Tom sympathetically, "I believe, if I had known all this, I'd have almost talked on the other side. At least, I wouldn't have tried to influence you any."

"But, my dear fellow, don't think you are the cause of all my doubts. You only echo to me what is in all the air; what learned books are saying. I have been thinking and studying this long while, and I am not afraid to face facts."

"And yet," remarked Tom, "the tragic side of these things comes over me sometimes as horrible. In a world like this, it costs fearfully to follow truth. The world has paid its pioneers and leaders generally with tombstones, after refusing them bread. Jesus said you couldn't follow him, in his day, without 'giving up all:' it's the same to-day."

"But, Tom, let's go home for some lunch. We've sat here long enough." And as they went down the bluff, and up the streets, they continued their conversation. At last, just before they got to his boarding-house, Mark said, —

"Well, of one thing I am sure: righteousness is better than unrighteousness; and, whatever becomes of the records, I believe in the ever-present spirit and the everlasting love of God. That's enough to preach for a while. I will busy myself in the practical work of trying to make my people better, and let the ferment of my mind work itself clear. So much is safe, any way."

IX.

A GAME OF CROQUET, AND WHO WON.

THE resolve at which Mr. Forrest arrived, at the close of the last chapter, gave him at least a temporary rest from his struggle with doubt. He had had hours when he had felt as though he could preach no longer. He seemed to be climbing the shifting side of a mountain of sand, that gave way at every step. He could find no solid place on which to plant his feet. And yet he must struggle on. He had left the quiet of tradition. He could not now go back, for he knew too much of the real uncertainty of those things that tradition takes for granted. The only course open was for him to press forward until he gained that other calm that comes of intelligent conviction.

But he could find — as others have done — a temporary peace by taking refuge in the practical, though he afterwards learned that no deep thinker can permanently rest so long as the theoretical and practical are out of harmony. But for the time he flung his doubts aside. He walked his study, and thought aloud : —

"Whatever else is doubtful, there is no doubt about the Golden Rule. What the world means by practical Christianity is practical righteousness; and by that law every intelligent man is bound.   Wherever it came from, whatever theory is held concerning inspiration, or the nature of Christ, on which it is supposed historically to rest, still Christianity is a fact.   And every man ought to be a practical Christian, because that means loving God and your fellow-men.   This, after all, is the heart of the whole matter; and in this spirit I will preach and work."

In such a mood it was easy for him to persuade himself that his theological troubles were, after all, not of chief importance, and that they did not necessarily touch the great essentials of life.   His natural temperament was buoyant and hopeful, and so he was inclined to make too little of a trouble that was past.   He even began to wonder that he had allowed it to trouble him so much.   And he sat down at his desk, and sketched a sermon for the next Sunday that he would preach "to doubters;" and in it he planned to take the ground, that, whatever theoretical difficulties any one might have, all were agreed that they should help build up "the kingdom of heaven" on earth, and that was the essential thing in religion.

He hardly knew it himself; and yet, to one who could have analyzed his motives, it would have been apparent that love was one of the main links of his logic.   "For, since these things are so," he thought, "I have been a fool to think I would be doing Miss Margaret a wrong to tell her of my love.   We shall be practically agreed in the work of life.   And if, as I cannot help hoping, she really cares for me, I might even be doing her an injury to turn away from her on account of a theological whim."

Do not blame him too severely, O reader, for his apparent inconsistency. Much may be forgiven to love. And, even if not, who of us but has sometimes seen the strong horse, Logic, harnessed in unconscious sophistries, and reined and driven by inclination?

Miss Margaret was now quite herself again. The wondrously beautiful autumn weather continued, a hazy, golden Indian summer, without a thought of chill in the balmy air. In front of the house was a narrow lawn, which extended widely on each side, and stretched far back at the rear. Tall elms and spreading chestnuts were scattered about irregularly, having the charm of native wildness, while the ground beneath was kept like a garden. Little lawn and croquet parties were common where the facilities were so tempting: so, on one of these fine autumn afternoons, Miss Hartley invited some of the young people of the society to tea, and to the croquet-matches that were to follow. Naturally Mr. Forrest was among the number. Being skilful in all games and out-door sports, having a ready fund of wit and anecdote, no such company was quite complete without him. And then it was proper and customary to invite the minister, particularly as he was young and single. We may guess, also, that possibly Miss Hartley may have had another and a more personal motive; for the young people — who have eyes for such things — had taken note of the fact that she seemed to take pleasure in his company; and aunt Sally Rawson had remarked in the sewing-circle, —

"I wonder if none on ye hain't noticed it. Sure's yer born, the minister's shinin' up to Judge Hartley's oldest gal;

and they say she 'pears to like it's well's he does.   Reckon
that's the reason he ain't called on me fer more'n a month.
I hope, when he gits settled down, he'll find time to 'tend to
his parish work a leetle better."

But, in blissful unconsciousness of sewing-circle criticisms,
Mr. Forrest accepted the invitation to the croquet-party.
Nor did he trouble himself about the motive that prompted
his invitation.   He was only too glad of any reason that
brought him near Miss Hartley; and he had already begun
to reproach himself that he had not made better use of his
opportunities at the readings, to find out whether his guesses
and hopes concerning her were true.

Tea passed, as such teas do, in pleasant chat about "airy
nothings;" except that now and then the judge tried, with
poor success, to give the conversation a theological turn, as
following the bent of his own inclinations, and what he also
considered the proprieties when a minister was present.   But
in the party of young and spirited people there was too
much of the flesh-and-blood life of this world to incline
them to take kindly to discussions about the other.

When tea was over they all adjourned to the lawn, some
to promenade and talk, some to sit under the trees and look
on.   The grounds were large enough to admit of several
croquet-sets, and so of several different parties at the play.
Mr. Forrest and Miss Hartley, well matched as to skill, were
among the best players on the grounds, and so were rarely
allowed to play together on the same side.

At last they had distinguished themselves so well, that
some one proposed they should play alone, one against the

other, for the evening's championship ; and gayly they entered
upon the pleasant contest. Mr. Forrest, being the stronger
of the two, might have had an advantage in striking, and
especially in croqueting his opponent's balls ; but of course
he was too chivalrous to take it. At the same time he considered it a poor compliment to her, and a real lack of
respectful courtesy, to give her a not-fairly-won game by
purposely playing poorly. So he determined to do his best.

They began, and played very evenly down the field to the
first stake ; and then, as they turned up on the home play,
a curious and superstitious feeling came over him, that somehow, as he struck the balls, he was driving about his own
destiny, and that winning or losing here was winning or
losing Miss Hartley forever.

There was something in the time and the air that helped
the weird sensation. It was now twilight, with a rising moon,
as yet behind an eastern hill, though its light was soft and
beautiful on the tops of the trees and the hills to the west.
And then his love for her was now grown so great that even
the slightest and most fanciful thing that in any way con-
nected itself with her relations to him took on a most exaggerated importance.

Lest his fancy should seem too fantastic, it will be well
for us to remember that there is something of the fetish-wor-
shipper still left in us all ; something of the feeling that in
the world's childhood, and among credulous and undeveloped people still, makes it easy to attach a magical and un-
reasonable importance to charms, to relics, and to fanciful
coincidences. When calm, and in daylight, many men and

women will laugh merrily over things, that, in reason's de-
spite, they pay a sort of superstitious regard to when nervous
or weary, or in the silence and weirdness of night.   People
still regard Fridays, and seeing new moons over left shoulders, and thirteen at table, who would be ashamed to defend themselves for doing it.   Dr. Johnson could bend all
his ponderous learning to a care to enter a room right
foot first, or to touching all the posts by the wayside with
his cane as he passed.   Byron's boldness became cowardice
when salt was spilled at table.   Similar whims or fancies
have their times of dominating us all.   Thus is our civilization still branded with the birthmark of the old world's
superstitions.

It must not be supposed that Mr. Forrest held his whim-
sical fancy as sober fact, even in his own mind.   Being
absorbed in the play, and musing and dreaming deeply of
his passionate love, he simply felt the fantastic spell of the
idea creep over him, and did not care to resist it.   He let
his weird fancy run on, and whisper to his anxious love that
he was playing for the high stake of her hand and the happiness of a life.   So he played in quiet and as if spell-bound.
He was proud that she played so well; and yet it was with
a sort of despair that he saw her take the lead.   And when
her ball passed through the last wicket, and rebounded from
the sharp stroke by which it was driven against the home
stake, so absorbed was he in his revery that he exclaimed, —

"Oh, heaven ! I've lost her !"

He had felt cut by a sharp pang at his heart, as though
some demonic power had seized her forever out of his sight.

He was really startled to find what an impulse he had felt to seize upon her before she should be spirited away. He looked about with some confusion as he became conscious of what he had said, and was relieved to see that only Miss Hartley had noticed his words. A strange look on her face made him think that she guessed the half-understood utterance had some reference to herself; but of course she made no allusion to it.

"Hurrah," said Miss Sue, "for the honor of our sex! Madge has won the game!"

"It's only a short-lived victory," said Miss Margaret; "for Mr. Forrest hasn't played his best to-night."

"Well," chimed in the other girlish voices, "we'll triumph while we may. A victory is a victory, for one night at least."

"A victory well earned," said Mr. Forrest. "No one shall dispute or deny the honors. Miss Margaret has the field; and to no other would I more readily yield up my mallet, and submit as the conquered must."

And so the playful chat went on. But soon the company had dispersed, all but Mr. Forrest and Miss Margaret, for Miss Sue had herself stepped into the house.

"Come, Miss Margaret," said Mr. Forrest, "the night is too lovely to go in as yet. Now that you have beaten me so badly, would it not be magnanimous in you to grant me a favor?"

"After my triumph, of course I ought to feel gracious and condescending. What favor?"

"A stroll over the hill yonder, toward the moon and the river. It is so mild, you cannot take cold."

"If you ask nothing harder than that, you will make it a pleasure to comply. I think, myself, it is too bad to lose an evening like this in the house."

And so through the moonlight and the shadows the two young and hopeful hearts went slowly up the sloping hill-side toward the east. The outer landscape of which they were a part was wondrously beautiful; but the inner world of high and pure imagination and brilliant hope, through which they moved together, was an enchanted land of romance and beauty. Is there any thing on earth so fair as the worlds that are created by youthful and pure love? He would have given all he possessed, to know that the fair creature beside him could find it in her heart to keep step with him on the pathway of life. And she — shall we reveal it? — knew, by her woman's instinct, that the strong and noble man by her side was her slave; but in her soul she looked up to him, and crowned him as the king of all the men she had ever seen.

They made a beautiful picture in the tender light. As the ascent of the hill grew steeper, she leaned happily upon his offered arm; and, though usually looking down or at the new scene of loveliness that opened at every step, now and then she stole a quick glance at his face, and tried to guess his thoughts. He was the image of strong, straight, and vigorous manhood. Her lithe and graceful form, covered but not concealed by the light crocheted shawl thrown loosely about her shoulders, was fit for a sculptor's model. Her dark eyes glowed in the shadow, or gleamed as the moonlight shone full in upon her face. He only wished such night and such companionship might never end.

"Miss Madge," said he, breaking the happy silence, —
"if I may dare to be so familiar," —

"Yes, call me Madge : I've often wished you would," said
she. "It brings back the old school-days, and makes me a
little girl again."

"And yet I wouldn't have you a little girl again."

"Why not?"

"Because you would not be what you are," he replied.

They now stood on the crown of the hill ; and they invol-
untarily stood still.

> "And this is in the night, most glorious night !
> Thou wert not sent for slumber !"

exclaimed Mr. Forrest. "Just see what a night, and what
a picture ! The city is now at our feet. See the sharp con-
trast of brilliant house-tops and dark-shadowed streets. How
still the busy life has become !"

"And the sky," said Madge : "it is so bright that hardly
a star dares try to rival the moon. How vivid those lines
of Wordsworth ! —

> 'The moon doth with delight
> Look round her when the heavens are bare.'"

"And only look at the river !" said he. "No one knows
how beautiful water can be till he sees it on such a night as
this. The high bank throws out there a ragged shadow ;
and all the rest is polished silver. The brown bluff yonder,
and the shadowy prairie beyond, make the contrasts perfect."

"Here, under these trees, are some rocky seats. Let's
sit down, and enjoy the scene for a little," said she.

When they were seated together Mark said, —

"It makes my heart ache still, to think what I suffered the last time I was as near to you as this."

"If proximity to me is painful, I will move," said she with an air of saucy banter.

"Now, it is too bad to torture my meaning so, even in fun," said he. "You can never know what I suffered."

"Why, how do you mean, and when?" said she, pretending an ignorance that was hardly real.

"Do you not know that I mean when I held your head on my knee, and watched in an agony of suspense to see your breath come back? I should have hated life unless you had breathed again."

He noticed that she blushed faintly in the moonlight as she said, —

"You did not tell me before that my head had been in your lap."

"But I had a right," said he in self-defence, "for I was your physician then."

He drew closer to her, and gently took the hand that lay in her lap, and which she did not withdraw.

"Madge," said he in a lower tone, "do you know, that, when you were unconscious, you called me Mark, and clung to me as if I were your protector?"

She did not answer, except by a far-away look in her eyes, and a hardly-perceptible flutter of her prisoned hand; and Mark continued, —

"And do you know, that, when the blood came back in your face, I was the happiest man alive? and that since that

time, whether looking at you in church, or walking or talking or reading with you, I have been trying to guess a
riddle that only you can answer, and that means life or
death to all I care for in the world?"

" Was it being absorbed in trying to guess that riddle, that
made you play so badly at croquet to-night?" said she.

" Did I play worse than usual?"

" Never so poorly, or I shouldn't have won. I know you
were dreaming, for you talked in your dream."

" O Madge!" said he, "it was a horrible fancy for a moment."

" What was horrible?"

" I thought I had lost — what was not mine to lose ; and
yet the wild fancy almost broke my heart."

" Why, what do you mean, Mr. Forrest?" said she, glancing in his face, and then quickly looking away again.

" I mean," said he passionately, "whatever I say, and
whatever I do, I mean always but one word : only that one
word is the universe to me : I mean — *love*, dear Madge !
Oh, do not speak at all, Miss Hartley, if you must say what I
dread ! and yet do speak ; for I cannot wait longer to know
if my dream is a lie."

She did not speak ; but, turning and looking up in his
eyes one moment, the tears started, and her head sunk on his
shoulder. He clasped her in his arms, and held her close
to his heart, both of them too happy to care for speech.
For perhaps it is true that two persons never know each
other perfectly till they can be completely happy in the mere
fact of companionship, without feeling the need of words.

What they said and did in the moments that followed, lovers need not be told, and others have no business to know. It was a beautiful world, of prairie and river and bluff and town, lighted by the moon, of which these happy lovers were a part; but within and before was a world that was fairer still, illumined with a light that "never was on sea or land." At last Mr. Forrest said, —

"Come, Madge, — for here I renounce the Margaret forever, — they'll be wondering what is become of us. We must return to the house."

And, as they went, the new love created for them a "new heaven and a new earth." They were new-born son and daughter of God, treading the fair, moon-kissed world, not envying even the angels; for were they not dwellers, too, in one of the starlit rooms of the divine house where the Father of both angels and men had given them their beauty and their bliss?

X.

THE MINISTER IN HIS WORK.

THE autumn flew on; for to Mr. Forrest its wings were well matched, love for his work, and love for Madge. His individual and private love, instead of hindering his universal, only broadened and deepened it, as giving him loftier and sweeter conceptions of the meaning and possibilities of human life.

Madge was troubled with only one thing, and this she did not reveal to him. Her father, the judge, when he learned of the engagement, gave a not over hearty consent. He was democratic enough to be willing to see her marry a man with no great means or high social position; but so intense was his dogmatic belief and zeal, that he would grimly have buried her, as though making her an offering to the Lord, rather than see her wedded to one with liberal — that to him meant infidel — tendencies. So he said to her, —

"I hope it will all turn out right, Margaret; but I fear, I fear. The best thinkers look upon our minister as dangerously tolerant towards error. He may come out of it; but, if not, it must not be. 'Be ye not unequally yoked together with unbelievers,' saith the Lord. So I charge you to use what influence you have over him, to keep him in the way of sound doctrine."

Margaret said not a word of this to Mr. Forrest, but only shut it up as a pain in her heart. For, while she loved him devotedly, she also idolized her father, and believed thoroughly in his opinions, knowing no reason why she should believe otherwise. While not lacking in intellect, but, on the contrary, having more than usual brain, she was yet, like most women, strongest on the side of sentiment, reverence, and love. She was not even familiar with theological distinctions, having no taste nor training that way. If she had seen a heresy, she would hardly have known it. And yet she was, by inheritance and training, thoroughly and strictly orthodox. She had been taught that all honest and sound thinking was the same. So, in her heart, she resented the imputation against Mark, as though his moral character or his mental ability had been impugned. If it were so, she could not love him less, but she would pity, and try to save.

But Mr. Forrest knew nothing of these things; and, for the time, he had flung his doubts and troubles aside.

As the weather grew cold, the religious fervor of the churches grew warm. To one who regards the natural philosophy of religious excitement and revival work, there is nothing strange in the fact that all revivals occur in the winter, and that they are most marked in times of popular depression; but from the supernatural standpoint it is a little puzzling to see why God doesn't "save souls" in the summer, and to trace the relation between the Holy Ghost and distress in the money-market.

But the time for the annual revival had come, and the churches set their machinery in motion. Mr. Forrest had no sympathy with what a famous orthodox professor once called " importing the Holy Ghost ; " believing, as he often said, that if God were not always present, and ready to help and save men from sin, then there wasn't any God.

So he organized his work after a different fashion. He believed in a present, living, loving God, who, any day or hour, was ready to help any man, high or low, who was ready to help himself. He believed in repentance and conversion as the manly recognition of evil in the life, and a resolute turning-away from that evil. He believed in the church as the banding together of true men for mutual religious help, and the purification and uplifting of society ; and in this spirit he labored. He saw no reason why men should not pay special and prolonged attention to these high matters of character, as well as to the work of carrying a political campaign.

Thus every evening, week after week, he spoke from his heart to a church full of attentive but rational and calm hearers. He labored to persuade men through their convictions ; naturally enough claiming, that, since men had brains, doubtless the Lord intended that they should use them concerning these grave affairs. Mr. Smiley was very much troubled at the class of men that came and listened ; and he was more troubled still, when they said that Mr. Forrest talked sense, and they were ready to be his kind of Christians. Even old Uncle Zeke came in, and dropped down on a back seat, and listened with open mouth, as though a new prophet had come.

Mr. Smiley put his arm through the arm of Deacon Putney, as they left the door of the church to go home one evening, and said, —

"Deacon, what do you think of the way things are going on?"

"Well," said the deacon cautiously, for he was not sure yet what others thought, "I have my times of hardly knowin'"—as though he ever had any other times: "what do you think?"

"I think this," said he, with great and unctuous positiveness: "that, when the unregenerate like a minister of the gospel, there is something wrong. 'The natural heart is enmity against God:' and, when the vital gospel is preached, the natural heart rebels. It don't look well to see lawyers and doctors, and so many moral men, present and approving. If they were on their knees and in tears, it would be another thing. But they simply listen and approve, and say, 'That is reasonable and right, and we ought to do it.' That ain't much like the preaching of Nettleton and Finney."

"Waal," broke in Uncle Zeke, who had come up behind on the sidewalk, and caught the last words, "what *would* ye like? ter hev 'em say they *don't* like it, and *won't* do it? Now, *I* call that preachin' a nat'ral and sensible religion. I'd like ter be that kin' o' Christian myself."

"Yes: that is the self-righteousness of a sinful heart," said Mr. Smiley. "The real gospel isn't natural, and men ought not to like it. Their stubborn wills should be broken, and they prostrated before the just wrath of an angry God."

"I don't go much fer breakin' folks's wills," said Uncle

Zeke. "Break yer mainspring, and then 'spect yer watch ter make time."

But as Mr. Forrest was making an undoubted success of his sensible and natural gospel, and as there was a prospect of a large addition of paying members to the church, the scruples gave way for the time, and he was allowed to "build up Zion" in his own way. For cavillers have sometimes noted the apparent fact, that the meshes of the sieve through which candidates for admission to the church are sifted have a somewhat peculiar way of expanding, and letting large but wealthy and respectable sinners through, while they automatically contract at the approach of social insignificance or questionable poverty.

At the other churches the usual drama was played. Mr. Forrest, one night at the close of his own service, stepped in at the —— church, to see the explanation of the strange hullabaloo that he heard. He knew they were sometimes noisy; but he thought something really unusual must this time have occurred. As he entered, a scene broke on him to which only the combined pencils of Doré and Hogarth could have done justice.

The minister stood inside the "altar." He had preached a sermon of great "unction," and wrought the people up to a pitch of intense excitement. His text had been, "How can ye escape the damnation of hell?" He had now come out of and before the pulpit, and was leading the "conference-meeting," and trying to gather in the fruits of his sermon. He stood with a glowing and exultant face, rubbing and occasionally clapping his hands, and now and again — when there was any appearance of lulling into quiet — shouting, " Glory ! " " Hallelujah ! " " That's good, brethren ! " " Praise the Lord ! " and other such phrases, to whip on the rushing excitement. He had just called on brother Baker to pray. The said brother happened to be in the back part of the house, and near to Mr. Forrest, who was by the door. The hubbub did not stop, nor did the minister even sit down or kneel. He seemed to be overlooking the field of action, like a general from a rising ground watching the progress of a battle. The irreverence of the whole thing to Mr. Forrest was such as to fill him with a shocking sense of disgust. Meantime brother Baker dropped on his knees, and began in so low a tone, that, in the general confusion, he could not be heard two pews away. Mr. Forrest caught his opening sentences, —

"O Lord ! we would not persume ter dictate, but we would humbly segest the perpriety of havin' a small bit of a revival in this place."

His voice went on rising and swaying until he fairly shrieked and screamed in his vehemence, —

" It is time for thee, O Lord, to work ! "

And now his yell — for it was nothing less — shrilled out above all the tumult ; and though two or three volunteers in other parts of the house had also begun praying at the same time, on their own account, he could still be heard above them all. He now gasped for breath : his hands clutched the seat, and the perspiration rolled from his forehead. Each separate word was a gasp ; and between them were interjected syllables, on which he seemed to rest for an instant while catching his breath for a still higher scream.

"O God-er, poor-er sinners-er droppin' into hell-er !
Shake-er 'em, Lord-er, and wake 'em up-er, to see-er the
gulf-er under their feet-er ! "

And, when no more breath was left, with one wild shriek
he gasped out "Amen ! " and rolled over on the floor.
And around swelled the chorus, "Amen ! " "Glory to God ! "
"Glory, glory, glory ! "

Then one of the brethren who recognized Mr. Forrest, and
wanted him to understand the spiritual artillery with which
his church was armed, touched him on the shoulder, and,
pointing to brother Baker's unconscious form, said, —

"Oh, but he's a mighty man at the throne of grace ! — a
powerful wrastler with the Lord ! "

"Yes," said another, " he jest storms the kingdom, and
brings the marcy down."

"And," remarked a third, " he's a wonderful pious man.
The trances and visions the Lord hez granted him is *re-*
markable.   He always goes off arter prayer."

Mr. Forrest inwardly thought that most people did "go
off" when they'd used up their limited supply of breath, but
he was too polite to say it.

But now their attention was turned another way.   By this
time several hysterical women were crawling about the aisles
on their hands and knees ; and several more were laid away
on the seats, having shouted till they too had " gone off," —
out of their senses in reality, but that here was supposed to
mean into heaven.   One enthusiastic brother now grasped
with both hands what he typically called the " horns of the
altar," but which, in reality, was the railing around the pul-

pit ; and, as he pulled and exhorted, a section of the " altar "
gave way.   He now seized one of the round, upright pieces,
— about the length and size of an ordinary cane, — and
while he shouted, —

"Flee, sinners ! flee for your lives into the ark !   The
storm is comin' : hasten while yet the door stands open !" —
he rushed wildly back and forth, punching in the ribs with
his stick the brothers and sisters that seemed indisposed
to hasten.

Mr. Forrest had now got all of this kind of religion he
could bear.   As he went out, he heard a drunken teamster,
who had run his wheel against a lamp-post, swearing at his
horse.

"Well," said he to himself, " I don't know which is worse,
the religious profanity inside, or the irreligious out.   What
strange ideas they must have about God, and the way to
please him ! "

XI.

UNDERGROUND RUMBLINGS.

MRS. GREY was a sore puzzle to the good church people of Bluffton. She was a widow of about forty-five years of age, well-preserved, and with a face singularly sweet and refined. Her hair, silvered as much with sorrow as with age, formed a saintly aureole about a face that pure thoughts, noble aspirations, and kindly deeds had sculptured into a more than fleshly beauty. She had come to Bluffton a few years before, hoping that a Western air would, if not restore to health, at least prolong the life of, a husband whose vitality was gradually burning away in the slow fire of consumption. She had watched and cared for him tenderly to the last. But when he had faded out of sight, instead of shutting herself up, and brooding over her own grief in the insidious selfishness of sorrow, she had said to Mr. Forrest, as he called upon her after the funeral, —

"I mustn't permit myself to brood here alone. I can't endure to sit still and only think of the past: it will distract me. Tell me what I can do. I can do no more for *him*. I can help the living, if I can't the dead."

And so she became a ministering angel. Having been

"made perfect through suffering," she carried with her the power of a genuine sympathy, that all the sick and poor could feel as a babe feels its mother's care, though they could not tell the tear-watered root from which it sprung. No one could help loving her. She was first in all the city work of benevolence; and her shadow, like Peter's in the Acts, was a shadow of healing wherever it fell.

Still, in spite of all this, — nay, because of all this, — she sorely troubled the church. Logically she *ought* to have been the worst woman in town. For — as was whispered about, and as was really true — she was an *infidel;* that is, she utterly rejected their church creeds and ways. It is well to note that the word "infidel" is one whose definition shifts according to geographical, social, and theological latitudes. Christians are all infidels to the Turks. Socrates was an infidel and an atheist in Athens. Galileo and Newton were infidels; and Darwin is still. So Mrs. Grey, though *faithful* to all known essential laws of God and man, was yet an "infidel" in Bluffton. Let us see some of her "strange peculiarities."

She would not go to church regularly, for the sake of going, and as a religious duty. She said, —

"I go to church to be fed. If there is nothing on the table, it seems to me a waste of time to sit down to it. I'll go to my own cupboard for crumbs."

And so she would search her small library for what she thought profitable as Sunday reading. She was not ecclesiastically strict on Sunday. She would even sew, if she found some poor family was suffering for work done. This strange conduct she justified by references to the ass in the pit in the Gospels, and the beasts led away to watering. She also said there was no command in the Bible, and no ground in history, for keeping any such idle Sunday as they claimed she ought. And, because they could not contradict her, they were all the more angry, and louder in their abuse. She did not believe in prayer either, as popularly understood. She said she did not believe in *teasing* God; and she thought it an imputation on his goodness to suppose he needed urging, and an insult to his intelligence to suppose he needed information. Prayer with her was only heart-communion, and was just as good when silent.

No wonder they called her names. It was the instinct of self-defence. For indeed the churches, as organized in Bluffton, had no excuse for existence if her ideas were true.

This, then, was the character that was "gone over" in the gossip of the sewing-circle.

"Well, now, I think it's jest a shame, Mis Howett," broke out old Mrs. Buck, "fer you to let your Looizer go 'round with Mis Grey so much."

"Pray tell me why," said Mrs. Howitt. Mrs. Howitt was a quiet, firm, ladylike woman, who, while evangelical, believed that a tree might safely be judged by its fruits; and she preferred a good apple grown on a heterodox tree to a rotten one whose trunk was orthodox.

"Why?" said Aunt Sally Rawson, "'pears as ef it needn't take long to know why. Don't the whole town know she's 'n infidel?"

"Yis; an' I think she's just splendid!" broke in the irrepressible Jane Ann Rawson.

"Jane Ann, speak when you're spoken to," said her mother. "Her insinuatin' ways is even leadin' my darter astray from the teachin's I give her in her childhood. That's what comes of sich examples as you set, Mis Howitt. Jane Ann sees Looizer with her, an' she follers on."

"But," said Mrs. Howitt, "what do you mean by her being an infidel?"

"Why," exclaimed Mrs. Buck, "she don't read the Bible; an' my old man said he saw a book onct on her table, that he thought looked like Tom Paine, — though I wouldn't hev you think he ever saw Tom Paine."

"An' that ain't all," said Aunt Sally: "she don't go to church; an' she scoffs at prayer-meetings."

"Well, I don't care 'f she doos," burst out Jane Ann again: "I think prayer-meetin's is just horrid!"

"Why, Jane Ann Rawson! I should think you'd be afeard the lightnin' 'd strike you. Don't you ever let me hear you speak like that agin."

"But," said Mrs. Howitt, "while I am sorry Mrs. Grey doesn't look at some things as we do, we must all confess that her life is a rebuke to the Christianity of all of us."

"Well, that won't never do," said Mrs. Buck: "I think it's all the worse. 'Twould be better for the community 'f she was a bad woman. When Satan comes as a angel o' light then look out for 'im, I say."

"Anyhow," said Jane Ann, "there's some folks in town that talks 'bout the 'higher life,' claims to be 'sanctified,' and says they hain't sinned fer a year, that would be might-ily improved to git a little o' her goodness."

"Jane Ann, who you squintin' at now?" inquired Mrs. Buck, with a severe tone of voice ; for she herself was among those who had "attained perfection."

"You needn't jump till yer hit," said Jane Ann, not over-respectfully. "I don't mean you. I do mean the Hinmans, though."

"Why, what o' them, I sh'd like to know? Mis Hinman's a saint. She don't do nothin' from mornin' to night 'cept go to meetin', an' pray."

"Yis, she do, though," said Jane Ann.

"What?"

"Why, nothin', only spin street-yarn, and let th' old man swear coz she hain't got dinner ready ; and Jim and Jake go cussin' round, out o' school, and their trousers all rags."

"And Mrs. Hinman's brother, another 'sanctified' one," said Mrs. Howitt, "and who says he hasn't had a sinful thought for six months, — he rents his stores for grog-shops, and has an agent run a house of bad repute for him. Now, ladies, if this is religion, I am seriously thinking of turning Mrs. Grey's kind of infidel."

"Well, 'f I ever did hear sich talk ! and from a church-member too ! No wonder your Looizer hain't got religion. Might know the Lord 'd pass by a house where sich senti-ments is believed in," said Mrs. Buck.

"When the Lord does come to my house, as you say, Mrs. Buck," remarked Mrs. Howitt, "I hope he'll not make my Louisa such a Christian as the Hinmans are."

"Mr. Forrest thinks Mis Grey's as good's a Christian, anyway," said Jane Ann.

"Yis, I've no doubt he doos," tartly replied Mrs. Buck, "and not much to his credit, neither. He's too much taken with Mis Grey's infidel notions, 'cordin' to my thinkin'."

"That's where ye're right, Mis Buck," said aunt Sally. "On'y last sabbath he had a hit agin people's goin to meetin' reg'lar; said some folks 't went to meetin' so much 'd better stay to home, and look after their fam'lies, do their duties, and pay their debts."

"Now, I call that infidel," said Mrs. Buck. "When a minister of the gospel gits to preachin' morality, then, I say, it looks like Unitarianism. I said to my old man on'y last Monday, sez I, 'John,' sez I, 'all this morality's well enough; but when I go to church, I go t' enjoy *religion*, an' I don't want no cold hashin' up er duties and sich stuff.'"

"But are there no duties and morality in religion?" inquired Mrs. Howitt. "For my part, I only wish Mr. Forrest could make all the church *live* as well as Mrs. Grey does."

Just at this point the door of the church-vestry opened, and in walked Mrs. Grey and Mr. Forrest. They had not come together, but had met at the street-corner. They looked about for a moment, and saw the usual scene. Here one or two ladies were standing at tables, cutting out garments; and, scattered in groups here and there, many others were sewing and chatting. Tongue and needle generally went together; but over at one side they noticed that the needles had stopped, and the tongues ran on alone. This was the place where was seated the little knot whose rather interesting conversation we have been overhearing.

The new-comers, recognizing Mrs. Howitt, stepped over to speak with her. All the rest also jumped to their feet with the most profuse demonstrations of pleasure.

"Why, Mr. Forrest, so glad to see you!" said Mrs. Buck.

"Yis; speak of angels, and they allus shows theirselves," exclaimed aunt Sally Rawson. "We's jest sayin' how the Lord was prosperin' his work, and buildin' up the walls of Zion. That sermon o' your'n last sabbath was jest bread from heaven."

"And, Mis Grey, how *do* you do? It's a long time sence we had the privilege o' seein' you 't our circle," said Mrs. Buck, as though she really meant it.

"We was jest a-sayin', Mis Grey," remarked aunt Sally, "how much the young gals o' the s'iety thinks o' you." She framed the sentence ingeniously, so as not formally to lie, while getting the advantage of the reality, — a popular device by which many suppose they keep on the side of truth. Neither Mr. Forrest nor Mrs. Grey said any thing worth our recording. They talked pleasantly and politely for a few moments, and then passed on to greet other acquaintances. As soon as they were out of hearing, Jane Ann exploded.

"If lyin's a proof of people's bein' 'perfected' and 'sanctified,' then I know lots o' folks that's in danger o' bein' translated 'fore they knows it," said she, in a tone of biting sarcasm.

Mrs. Buck's hands went up in horror.

"Sich impidence and sich impiety I never did hear," she exclaimed. "This is what comes o' Mis Grey's influence, an' Mr. Forrest's lettin' down the tone o' his preachin'."

"Jane Ann, you put on yer things, and go right straight home. I'll have a season o' prayer with you 'fore you go to bed. I wonder the Lord don't smite ye for sech talk," said her mother.

"'F the Lord *should* go to smitin', some other folks might git hit," muttered Jane Ann under her breath, as she departed.

Mrs. Howitt now left them; and they had an edifying talk on the condition of parish affairs, garnished with sundry choice bits of scandal that seemed equally as dear to them as did the state of religion.

When they had gone the rounds, Mrs. Grey said to Mr. Forrest, —

"Are you engaged this afternoon?"

"Not so but that I am at your disposal," said he.

"If, then, you have no objection, I'd like a little talk with you."

"Will you go to my study?"

"No, if you please. You come up to my house. It will do you good to get out of your parish atmosphere for a little."

XII.

MR. FORREST AND MRS. GREY.

MRS. GREY'S small, neat house was on a slope of the hill overlooking the town. From the little bay-window where Mr. Forrest sat in a cosey rocking-chair, he could see the river on one side, the uneven but beautiful and tree-crowned ranges of hills back of the city, while the city itself made a picture in the foreground.

"There," said Mrs. Grey, pulling the curtains clear up so as to give an unobstructed view in all directions, "we are here raised, at least in space, above the petty superstitions, the unreasoning traditions and narrow views, of the thoughtless mass that makes up the town below us."

"If elevation in space," said he, "was only intellectual elevation, I would certainly try to get them all to build on the hills."

"But," said she, "you'll forgive me for speaking plainly; you know me well enough now to understand me: do you think you are doing all you might to help them?"

"I mean to.   Where do I fail?"

"Will you pardon me if I tell you?"

"Certainly.   Why not?"

"Well, I believe you will. If I didn't believe in you, I shouldn't talk at all. And you know I look upon you as a sort of boy of mine. And I don't think you ought to be where you are."

"But you said you'd tell me where I failed."

"I think," said she slowly, and looking him full in the face, "that you are not quite frank enough."

"You don't think I deceive my people?"

"Not consciously or purposely, by any manner of means; but, really, yes."

"Pray tell me wherein."

"Well, the atmosphere you breathe is not a natural, healthy one."

"Explain."

"Why, you are not orthodox. I feel it every time I hear you preach. That in you which touches and moves men is your heresy. Of course I rejoice in it; and I hope much for you when you once get where you belong. But you ought to be orthodox, or you ought not to hold your position. Every time you rise and stand in your pulpit, your people think that means that you believe things that I know you are too intelligent to hold."

"Perhaps I'm not so intelligent as you suppose. So I may believe more than you think I do."

"May I catechise you a little?"

"Nothing would suit me better. I like to talk these things over; and you know me well enough to know that I haven't any beliefs I prize so much as I do the simple truth."

"I believe it, and therein is my hope for you. If it were not so, you would not have dared to have preached what you already have."

"Do you think I've really gone far out of the way of 'sound doctrine'? I haven't thought of being brave, for I have only spoken what seemed to me simple reason and truth."

"That's your offence. They don't want you to preach reason. I'm aware that the majority of the church like you, for they do not think deeply on theological points. But the leaders don't; and, as sure as the world, there's trouble brewing. Your being my friend is a crime. That you study and read science, is against you. Things are not going as they are now for a great while."

"Well, let it come if it must. But the catechism?"

"All right, then. Last Sunday you closed your prayer with the words, 'For Christ's sake.' Why?"

Mr. Forrest thought a moment, and then answered frankly, "Training and habit, perhaps; for I am aware the phrase has no New-Testament authority."

"And did you never think the implication is almost impiety? It is a figure borrowed from the habits of Oriental courts and despots. When the sultan will not grant a favor for the suppliant's need's sake, or because it is beneficent or right, still he sometimes will for the sake of a court favorite. Do you think God is that kind of a being?"

"I fear I never thought of its implication before."

"Well, do you think Christ has any thing to do with our prayers, any way?"

"Only this: I do think he is the manifestation of that character and disposition, on the part of God, that invites our prayers."

"You do not, then, hold that Christ's death as a sacrifice has any thing to do with God's ability or willingness to hear prayer, and forgive sin?"

"Indeed I do not. That was only an *expression* of an eternal willingness. I could not love a being whose nature it was not to save."

"You are aware, I suppose, that these views are not quite consistent with the old ideas of the Trinity?"

"Yes; and for that, I confess I don't much care. I'm not the only orthodox minister who doesn't believe the Trinity."

"How do you hold things, then?"

"Well, something like this. The doctrine of the Trinity is utterly meaningless. I can't even understand its terms."

"Perhaps I'm not theologian enough to understand what those terms are."

"These, then: I am expected to believe that God is three persons, and am told in the same breath that the word 'person' doesn't mean person, but something else. I ask what else, and nobody knows. Then these three persons are only one person. I have asked a great many laymen to tell me what the Trinity is, and I have never found one who could do it. They always give me Unitarianism in some form, or Tritheism. And I don't wonder."

"What, then, do you believe?" said she.

"I believe in the universal and omnipresent God, who is

a spirit. That's the first person. Christ, to me, is only a manifestation of this unseen spirit in the sphere of humanity. The Father, as a separate personality, nothing."

"You say you are not the only orthodox minister who holds such views?"

"I have a good deal of company. It isn't much wonder if many people are a little mixed over what nobody can understand."

"But how can you claim to be orthodox?"

"Why," said he, "I follow Jesus. He never claimed to be God."

"How about 'I and my Father are one'?"

"But right in immediate connection he prays that the disciples may be one with him *as* he is one with the Father. If one verse makes him God, the other makes all the disciples God as well. It proves too much."

"I am glad to hear you say it. But what of the first chapter of John? Do you think that teaches it?"

"I used to, but I know better now. Even if it did, it would only prove that the unknown author of John *believed* it, not that it is *true*. It is only the opinion of the writer, at best. But it doesn't mean that."

"What does it mean?"

"It means," said he, "a mystical, metaphysical notion of the Gnostics. They held to all sorts of gods and semi-gods, æons and emanations, to bridge over the gulf between God and matter. The New Testament's later documents are full of the technical terms of Gnosticism, showing how much that philosophy influenced the writers."

"But they say that Christ is spoken of as the creator of the world, and that only God can create."

"The Gnostic belief of the writer was the precise opposite. This sect held that the supreme God was too high and pure to come into contact with matter, and so did not and could not create the world. They taught that the world was created by a being they called the Demi-urgus, and whom they identified with Christ. To call Christ creator, then, was the most forcible way of saying he was *not* God."

"The genealogical tables of the Gospels have always surprised me, Mr. Forrest."

"Well they might. They do not agree with each other, nor with the Old-Testament tables; and, since they trace Jesus back to Joseph, of course have nothing whatever to do with him unless Joseph was his father."

"How do you account, then, for them as they stand?"

"Oh! they are part of an older tradition, that had changed its form by the time the Gospels came into their present shape. The old tradition was, that Joseph was his father, and the Holy Ghost his mother."

"How strange!"

"No, not strange. It was common enough in ancient times for men to believe in superhuman births, where either father or mother was divine."

"But isn't it remarkable that we know no more of the childhood of Jesus?"

"I think not: we know but *very* little about him anyway. We do not know when he was born, nor when he died. The Gospels disagree as to the length of his ministry, one making

it three years, the rest one; and John seems to imply that
he lived till he was on toward the age of fifty. But, if we
had known all about his childhood, we should never have
had the dogma of the incarnation. There must be mystery
and uncertainty to give room for the imagination to create
myths."

"It seems so strange that men can believe that God was
ever born as a man!"

"Yes, just think of it! — God born a baby, puling, whin-
ing, crying in the arms of a nurse; God going to school, and
getting his lessons; God sitting at the feet of quibbling, hair-
splitting rabbins in the synagogue, and learning his own law.
It seems blasphemy to me sometimes. It was easy enough
to think such childish thoughts when men thought the universe was only a little three-story house, with hell for cellar,
and heaven for upper story. God could then come down
stairs, and see what was going on, disguising himself in a
human body. But, in our present knowledge of the universe,
it is most stupendous absurdity to think such things."

"But these ideas are not altogether ancient, are they?"

"No: in certain grades of civilization it seems easy to believe such things. Within fifty years some of the tribes of
India have deified, and are now worshipping, an English
officer."

"But you just referred to hell as the 'cellar' of the old
universe. I have noticed you do not preach it; and this, I
understand, is one ground of parish complaint."

"This is a horrible subject to me, Mrs. Grey. Oh, what a
childhood it gave me! However beautiful the day or the

landscape, or however joyous the plays, this haunting horror used to come to blot out the light, and make me tremble. A blue sky, fields full of flowers, and — hell ! what a mixture for childhood ! And if ever, during boyhood, there was a fire, a house burnt, you cannot imagine what I suffered. I feared I was not one of the 'elect ; ' and I saw myself livid and red-hot, and writhing in the flames. And it was — *forever!* Oh, how I used to rush home, and bury my face in the bed-clothes, to try to shut out the inner vision, and then at night cry and shiver myself to sleep ! "

" When did you cease believing it ? "

" I hardly know as I have ceased believing it yet, in some form. My views have changed greatly with more study and thought, since I came to Bluffton. The first thing that fairly started my thinking on the subject was a tract I once came across. I was trained as a child to think Universalism synonymous with every thing evil. And, indeed, the old form of Universalism now seems to me the height of absurdity. I can't believe that any magic at death can make all souls, so unlike five minutes before, equally fit for heaven five minutes after."

" But what of this tract ? "

" I got hold of it somehow, and read it in my study in California. What an agony of mind I went through ! I wanted so to believe it ! One moment I would ; and then my heart burst out singing ; and all the world seemed to break forth in glad rejoicing that hell was no more. And then I dared not believe it. It was Satan tempting me. I was being led astray. I was falling over into an abyss. The mental struggle was awful.

"But though I did not accept the teaching then, for fear I was going astray, it had started thoughts that would not rest. I felt impelled to re-examine the grounds of the belief."

"Well, what have you found? For, though the teachings of all the Bibles in the world couldn't make me believe it, yet I like to know how it lies in other thoughtful minds."

" In the first place, I have gone over the Bible as bearing on the subject; and I am surprised to find how large a part of the common belief is based on ignorance, mistranslation, and change in the meaning of words. For instance, there isn't a trace of everlasting punishment in the Old Testament. Indeed, the Jews had no fixed or clear belief in a future life at all. It was a late growth, and largely received from the Persians at the time of the captivity. So there is not one single place in the Old Testament where 'hell' means hell as the word is used to-day. It is false to honesty and the Bible itself, to let the word stand there. And then, leaving out repetitions of the same sayings in the different Gospels, there are no more than six places in the New Testament where the word 'hell' ought to be in the text, even if it ought to be there at all. As to these six, it is simply begging the question to say that the original 'Gehenna' means what we mean by hell."

"But, though I do not believe it any the more for that, it seems to me the Bible teaches it. It says everlasting punishment, and everlasting life, putting the two on the same level."

"Begging your pardon, no. The word, *aionios*, is used

many times where it doesn't and can't mean everlasting. The true translation is *eternal;* but the word does not determine the duration, referring sometimes rather to quality and kind than quantity, and in any case leaving the term indefinite."

"But you say you still believe it."

"Not *everlasting:* I cannot. I believe in *future* punishment. For the same laws of right and wrong, of reward and penalty, are everywhere. Results, good or bad, inevitably attach themselves to our deeds, and must do so always and everywhere."

"Do you believe man is too good to be punished forever?"

"I'd rather say, I believe he is not bad enough to be punished forever. It seems monstrous injustice. No man, in a long life, could commit crimes enough to deserve it."

"But you know it is often said, that the man will keep on sinning, and so will keep on suffering."

"Not if God is king, and can have his own way. The worst of the whole doctrine is its blasphemy toward God. He either can, or can't, *some time* save all. If he can't, he isn't God; for his power is limited. If he can, and will not, then he's no God, but a devil."

"But, they say, he is limited by man's free-will, and must let him take his own course."

"I know that is urged; but it is a quibble. We talk much of human obligation : isn't there any *divine* obligation? I say it reverently; but God has no right to create a cause that he cannot control, and that he knows will result

in evil. To do so would make the evil his own. It is so
simple a principle of justice, that all human laws recognize
it concerning human actions. The creation of the world, if
its outcome is to be irremediable evil to a single human soul,
is a gigantic crime. For even God has no right to do other
than right. And what would be a crime on earth can't be
goodness in heaven."

"With such beliefs as these, how can you remain in an
orthodox church?"

"I wake up and find these things forcing themselves on
me in the orthodox church, and I do not as yet see my way."

"Go into another church."

"Where? I am not a Universalist. I am not a Unitarian. Both hold beliefs I cannot accept. Neither of their
systems will be the church of the future. There is nowhere
to go. I have plenty of company. Other ministers are in the
same position. And yet I stay so far, more because I know
not how to leave, than because I think I ought to stay."

"But you do not preach what you do not believe? I
can't think that of you."

"Never. I simply keep still concerning my doubts. I
preach positively what I do believe, — the great principles
of righteousness, the central ideas of a Christian life."

"Well, Mr. Forrest, I think I feel the difficulties of your
position. And I fear your enemies, that smile upon you,
will help you settle the question."

"I am ready to face whatever comes."

But, as he walked toward his study, he said to himself, —

"Can I face *all*?"

XIII.

A SOUL COME TO JUDGMENT.

FROM the sitting-room of Mrs. Grey, Mr. Forrest went alone to his study.

The great battles of the world are fought alone. Before men appear in the great crises of the world, to head forlorn-hopes, guide nations, or lead others to victory, they have first met, fought, and conquered themselves, on the unseen battle-fields of the soul. There is no shouting, no noise of cannon, no waving of flags above the smoke; but only a cry of prayer, or a sigh of agony breathed out, that, like the puff of steam from a volcano, tells of the infernal strife below. It is the Armageddon battle-field, where the hosts of good and evil clutch in deadly encounter. He who has won here is safe. No other is fit to trust as leader when grand human destinies are hanging in the balance. Here Moses, and Sakya-muni, and Jesus, and Mohammed, and Luther, and Wesley, and Channing, and Parker fought, and raised their monuments of triumph. Here all true souls are tested. This battle is the soul's crisis or judgment-seat, in the true New-Testament sense.

It is the man's ordeal, through which he passes while above him "the throne is set, and the books are opened."

Here, then, is Mr. Forrest come at last. He had caught glimpses of the gathering hosts before. He had already been in the edge of the fray more than once, but had withdrawn again, and postponed the decision. But now he neither could nor cared to escape. His conscience sounded the bugle, and he prepared himself for the issue. He felt he was fighting for the prize of his own soul. His manhood was to be lost or won. The combatants are to be found in every live and earnest human heart. Progress fought reaction; freedom struggled with tradition, and bondage to the letter of other men's thoughts; honesty was matched against a compromising conformity; the faith of Abraham, that "went out, not knowing whither," — only knowing that God had called, — was met by the timidity that doubted whether God ever led into new lands; worldly favor sought to seduce the loyalty that prompted to choose duty at the cost of any loss; a passionate love sought to make duty conform to its own sweet interests; while reverence for the past tried to make his independent search seem a traitor to the ancient wisdom that claims with authority to represent God.

Well may you offer him your sympathy; for it was a Gethsemane struggle. He would almost rather have died than enter the battle. And though he should struggle, and come off victor, still he felt that it must be at such a cost as might leave him stripped of all he cared to live for. So it was the bitterness of death on either hand.

He sat down at his desk, rested his elbows on its top, and

his temples on the palms of both his hands, and listened to the cries that came up from the deeps of his soul.

"O God!" he cried, — "if there be a God, — why must one so doubt and suffer in trying to find thee, and the way of thy truth?"

And then he sat, and thought over the pathway of human progress, and noted how it was tear-sprinkled and blood-marked all the way.

"It has been one long martyrdom," he said. "From the dwellers in caves, clear on, it has been one long agony and martyrdom. Only they who have been willing to be useless, to live lives of mere animal content, have been comfortable. The thinkers, the inventors, the prophets, they who have tried to give something to mankind, have been like Prometheus, — have paid for it by endless vulture-gnawings at their vitals."

Here he sprang to his feet, and walked the room. And out of his terrible doubt he exclaimed, —

"Can it be, after all, that the eternal God is only a Jove-like tyrant, jealous of man's welfare, and so torturing those who would be his benefactors, leading to higher thoughts and better ways? If not, why are the prophets cast out? why do they have to pay, in tears and torture, for the help they would render their fellow-men?"

"But this," he continued aloud, "is blasphemy. 'Shall not the Judge of all the earth do right?' There could be no sense of right at all, were God not righteous. That the universe is orderly at all, proves that order rules. That there is any moral order, proves right supreme. And yet the price of it! Could not the pain be spared?"

Then he caught up his New Testament, and read how Jesus, "though he were a son, yet became perfect through the things that he suffered." But, as he mused, he said, —

"But this does not make it seem right. It only shows that the greatest souls are subject to the inevitable law."

And then he turned to "In Memoriam," and read, —

> "I falter where I firmly trod,
>   And, falling with my weight of cares,
>   Upon the world's great altar-stairs
> That slope through darkness up to God, —
>
> I stretch lone hands of faith, and grope,
>   And gather dust and chaff, and call
>   To what I feel is Lord of all,
> And faintly trust the larger hope."

"After all," he said, "whatever is dark, there is no doubt, that, if I am to be a man, I must hear and obey my conscience, and not falter when duty calls. They who die for right are victors, though they go down into the dust and endless night; and they who live, and pay their manhood for the privilege, are buried forever beneath the *débris* of their own souls."

This point of the battle, then, he had won. He would be true to himself at any cost.

"But I'm not true to myself," he exclaimed, "so long as I occupy this equivocal position. I must leave Bluffton. I go and stand in my pulpit, and feel that I am acting a lie. I am understood to be orthodox: my standing there proclaims the fact. I can't endure it! I shall get so that my soul will consent to be false; and then what shall I be worth to anybody? Since all things are so uncertain, I almost wish I had never thought and studied. But I *have* thought and studied, and the fate is on me."

And then came the tempting suggestion,—

"But the most of your people like the doctrine you preach; and you can mould them to your will. The few who oppose, you can drive away, and have the field to yourself."

It was a sweet thought for a moment, and he almost yielded. Then he trembled to think what traitor forces were in him; and an imagination a little more vivid would have made him fling his inkstand, like Luther, at the haunting devil of deceit.

"Yes, of course I *might* do it, if I could play an underhand game like that. I know they like my doctrine; but they would not if they knew its name. When I lead churches into new truth, I will do it with open colors, and not in uniforms that are stolen."

While he had walked his study, and thought, and read, and struggled, the twilight had come on. The tea-bell rang, but he sent down word that he would not eat to-night. Then he went to his window, and looked out to the east, and saw that the moon was rising. It threw a bridge of silver beams across the river, as fair as the streets that the angels tread. And then his eyes wandered over to Madge's window; and his heart beat wildly at the thought of her womanly beauty and his great love.

"O Madge!" he cried, "you little know the bitterness

that comes to my heart as I think of your sweet love. But
I can endure this here no longer. I must get out into the
night."

He caught his hat, and started for the hills. He walked
for an hour with no other purpose than to do the impossible, — get away from himself. At last the attraction of the
spot and the memory of that night brought him to the place
where Madge's silence had confessed her love. He sat
down, and looked about him. The picture of ragged bluffs,
and wide river, and starry sky, brought to his thought those
lines of Byron : —

> " 'Tis midnight : on the mountains brown
> The cold, round moon shines deeply down.
> Blue roll the waters ; blue the sky
> Seems, like an ocean hung on high,
> Bespangled with those isles of light
> So wildly, spiritually bright.
> Who ever looked upon them shining,
> And turned to earth without repining,
> Nor wished for wings to flee away
> And mix with their eternal ray ? "

"They look peaceful," thought he ; "and ever since man
suffered they have tormented him with the spectacle of their
inaccessible peace. But now even the dream of *their* peace
is gone. The suns are torn with storm and tempest compared with which our earthly tornadoes are quiet. And our
modern knowledge tells us that the most distant planets are
like our own old earth, upheaved with earthquakes, and torn
with volcanic fires. And the inhabitants are doubtless like

us. Perhaps on Venus yonder (to whose people our earth is the most beautiful planet in heaven) some man like me may be looking up to the earth, and longing for the peace and beauty that appears to be our lot. There is no longer refuge in the stars. Each must fight his own battle for himself, and find heaven or hell where he is."

And then his thought turned to his love; and he meditated, —

"It were easy enough to fight the battle, if you were not involved in it, Madge. It isn't easy to turn one's back on friends and old associations, — to have those who love us think we have given up God, and fallen forever into the hands of evil. But all this could be borne. But to pain *your* heart, perhaps — to *lose* you! O Madge, I can't endure it!"

For he had learned so much of her nature, and knew her past training so well, that he feared her sense of duty — which was no less strong than his own — might make her sacrifice even her love, though at the price of desolating her life, rather than yield to what she had always been taught to hate and fear as the enemy of God. And it was just this grand heroism of her character that made him admire her. She was of the same moral fibre as the judge, her father. She would have been a martyr, and sung and gloried in the flames, in the days when such things were. And her love only intensified this. She loved as passionately as she worshipped: only the love and the worship must not conflict. And Mr. Forrest saw, with admiration mingled with terror, that her present light would drive her very noblest qualities into opposition to the now roused sense of duty in his own soul. It would be conscience against conscience, — God against God.

"And herein," he said, "is the tragedy of duty. What shall become of poor, weak, human hearts between two such forces, neither of which can give way? And yet, O God! I must be true, though it means being 'damned for thy glory.' I shall lose her, if I am true ; and yet, if I am not, I shall not be fit to win her. Charybdis and Scylla, on one of you I shall wreck."

He now rose again, but could not bear to go into the house. He was in no mood for sleep. He wandered and thought till he found himself on the summit of Bowman's Hill, above the calm river that held the stars on its bosom. He looked over toward the cottage ; and there was uncle Zeke, leaning over his fence and looking up at the sky, as though he had come out for a breath of fresh air before going to bed.

"Uncle," said Mr. Forrest "it looks peaceful up there. I wish the world was as quiet as the heavens seem to be."

"Why, Mr. Forrest ! what's turned you into a night-walker? Folks ain't gin'ally trampin' round up here at bedtime."

"Well, I'm restless, and don't feel like sleep."

"In love, mebbe. I was in love onct ; but " (rubbing his eyes with his rough fist) "she died, and I never cared for nobody else. But when I fust loved, and before the shadder come, I used to couldn't stay in the house sech nights as this ; used to wander round, and think how much more light ther' wuz in her eyes fer me than there wuz in all the stars."

By this time uncle Zeke and Mr. Forrest were fast friends. The old man had found in the new minister a touch of fresh, true manhood, and a rational view of religion, that won his respect, and now he would have done any thing for him that a Newfoundland would have done for his master; and Mr. Forrest found in him a bit of true and sound wood, though gnarly in the grain, that gave him a new respect for the raw material of healthy human nature.

So, though he did not resent the reference to his love, the subject was too sore and sacred to be handled by any human touch; and he therefore waived the point, and simply said,—

"I'm thinking, uncle Zeke, that I'll have to leave Bluffton."

"Why, you only come in June; and now it's jest gittin' well on into spring. Not a year yet. What do you mean?"

"I mean, I can't stay, and be an honest man."

"Why, Mr. Forrest, I'se goin' ter say you's a'most the only honest man here; an' you oughtn't to talk o' goin'."

"But what if I can't be honest if I stay?"

"Your remarks is way off color to me. I don't sense what yer drivin' at."

"Well, I'm driving at this. The church is orthodox. You know I am not,—or you wouldn't like me as I think you do,—and so I am where I do not belong. Does it look clear now?"

"Yis, Mr. Forrest, it doos; clearer'n I wish it did. You know how I've larned to like you; an' you've throwed light fer the fust time on tough things that used ter trouble me.

You know," he huskily added, for his voice was getting low
in his throat, " I told yer I liked the looks o' ye, the fust time
I sot eyes on ye that Sunday mornin' arter you come by the
boat; and I know how the pious cusses — beg parding, Mr.
Forrest, but I can't help it — are raisin' a rumpus behind
yer back.   I knowed a fuss was comin'.   But can't ye fight
it out, and stay ? "

" But I ought not to stay in an orthodox church if I don't
belong there."

" No more ye'd ought," said uncle Zeke, " though it tugs
a mighty heap at my heart to say so.   'Twill be orful lonesome.   An' yit I shouldn't 'spect you ef you warn't true to
yer convictions ; coz that's what I take to yer fur."

If Mr. Forrest had had any hesitation, the re-enforcement
of uncle Zeke's simple clear-headedness would have given
his conscience the victory.

But as he turned to go back to his study, uncle Zeke said
cheerily, —

"Well, Mr. Forrest, mebbe 'twon't come to that now.
They may have sense 'nough to own up you're right, and
change ter your platform.   But ye'll be a man, anyhow."
And, as he wrung his hand with a hearty but rough grip, he
added, " God bless you ! God bless you !   The world's big,
my dear boy; an' somewhere ther's folks that'll listen to
you, though I'll be hungry for a relig'n 'thout the brains
out on't.

" But 'tain't come yit; and p'raps ye'll see yer way out
now."

The ordeal was over ; and the recording angel had written

it down, that another soul had stood before the eternal judgment-seat, and passed among those who were on the right hand of the Judge.

And, as Mr. Forrest walked home, his heart was as quiet as the stars appeared, though still a sadness, like a minor chord in music, made itself heard in the song of triumph that the angel thoughts sung in his soul.

XIV.

THE OFFENCE.

IT was now toward the first of May. What with private thought and study, with regular preaching, and the extra labor of the revival season; with parish work, and efforts among the poor; with the endless routine, and the thousand and one calls that come to the man who is everybody's servant and who yet is generally regarded as having nothing to do, — Mr. Forrest found himself much worn, and needing, if no more, a brief rest. A little matter of business also required his attention. And, besides this, it seemed to him that the change of a short trip among new scenes might help clear his head, and strengthen his right resolves, after the internal ferment he had passed through. Who knew but something might occur to open a way for him out of his present wilderness?

It being now for some time well known that he was engaged to Miss Margaret, he was accustomed to spend much of the little leisure he had by her side. He forgot all evil and trouble in the light of her face. With her he was in paradise; and only when he left her did he go out and down into the confusion and struggle of life. But, when he was out, the thought that some day he might be shut out, and see only the cherub and flaming sword forbidding entrance again, made him faint and sick at heart.

He could hardly bear to leave her long enough for his contemplated trip.

" Madge," said he, as he stood by her side at her window, looking out on the fresh spring morning, " I can't bear to be away from you long enough for this trip. I feel as though some horrible power were waiting to steal you from me as soon as I am away."

" Why Mark, what a sickly fancy ! That very feeling is a reason why you should go. It's because you are nervously worn with your work. You'll come back with the clouds all out of your brain."

" You want me to go, then ? "

" Please don't be cruel, Mark. You know how I love to have you near me. But I love you enough to want you away when duty calls, and it is for your good."

" Two weeks seems so long now ! "

" I shall indeed be homesick for you. But think of me as happy and glad for you, and as looking East till you are West again."

He drew her to him, smoothed a loose lock of hair on her forehead with his hand, and then, lifting her fair round face till it looked in his own, gazed long and lovingly in her eyes, and kissed her a passionate good-by.

Little did he dream, in spite of his words of foreboding to Madge, that his trip to New York was to be the rising of a little cloud out of the east, that, gathering blackness, was to spread west, and darken all his horizon.

It is no part of our purpose to describe his journey, what he saw, said, or did. He looked after his business affairs : he visited several friends, one an old physician, at whose house he spent several days. When he returned, he had in his care a stranger, a lady, whom he left at the house of his friend Mr. Winthrop, at Maple City. There was much confidential talk between him and Tom ; but nothing that, as yet, we have any right to overhear.

Before Mr. Forrest left Bluffton, the excessive heat that in spring visits these low-lying river towns had already raised the fear of a coming epidemic. Occasional cases of cholera had been heard of in towns farther down the river. And now the hot May, combined with the lack of any proper sanitary care, had prepared a way for it at Bluffton.

At its first appearance, many of those who could afford to do so left the place. Or those who lived on the hills, where the air was pure, shut themselves in their homes, and left the town to shift for itself. As usual in such cases, those most exposed, living in the lower and poorer parts of the city were unable either to flee, or to defend themselves where they were : so the disease cut them down. The physicians stood bravely at their posts ; but their great difficulty was to get any one to nurse and look after their patients. The fear of the ravager drove even family friends and relatives into the selfish struggle to save themselves.

But a few heroic souls remained, and, passing from one house to another, did what they could for the dying, and helped pay the last rites for the dead. Among the foremost of these was Mrs. Grey. She was everywhere the tireless watcher and nurse, night as well as day. Mr. Smiley remarked to a friend, —

"I have no doubt this is a judgment of God on the wickedness of the city; and it isn't for us to interfere. When he has taken vengeance, he will stay his hand."

And he sent a note to Mrs. Grey, one extract from which read as follows : —

"You know I have always been interested in the welfare of your soul. You have been an infidel, and a scoffer at the ordinances of God; and I warn you not to peril your life in this way until you make your peace with him."

She sat down where she was, beside a sick-bed, and, turning the note over, she wrote on its back, and returned it with these words : —

"You think this is a supernatural judgment of God on the wicked. Unless, then, you regard yourself as one of the wicked, and liable to its stroke, why do you not leave the safety of your hillside, and come down and help us? Do you think God cannot smite the hill, or that he cannot keep you here? I think it the natural result of the ignorance and filth of the people. But, though they have brought it on themselves, still I must help them what I can. I haven't time now to 'save my soul:' I am too busy saving the bodies of others. Would it not be well for you to read the words of him you regard as God? — 'He that saveth his life will lose it; and he that loseth it for my sake will save it.'"

He was astonished, and felt insulted, at an "infidel's" daring to rebuke him, the leading man in the church. But she went on with her work.

But the prolonged watching, and the breathing of the malarious air, were telling upon her. And when the epidemic began to abate, and when she thought her labors were well-nigh over, she awoke to a recognition of the symptoms in herself; and, the very morning on which Mr. Forrest returned from New York, she was carried to her hillside cottage, to pay the penalty of her devotion with her own life.

Uncle Zeke met Mr. Forrest at the levee; and, as he grasped his hand, he said, —

"Bad news for ye, Mr. Forrest. She's jist ben an angel while ye ben gone; and now she's took."

Mr. Forrest had learned of the epidemic; but not having heard of Madge since leaving New York, his first thought was of her; and he exclaimed, —

"Who, Uncle Zeke? Miss Hartley" —

"No, no: Miss Hartley is well, though she's done all she could. But Mrs. Grey is took, and I'se afraid for the wust."

"But where is she?" he hurriedly inquired.

"They've car'ed her home," said he.

"Thank you, uncle, for telling me. I must go to her at once."

And before going even to speak to Madge, he hastened to the house of Mrs. Grey. He found his worst fears justified. She was sinking rapidly. Her face lighted with joy and welcome as he went in, and took her hand, already clammy and cold.

"O Mrs. Grey!" he exclaimed, while the tears blinded his eyes, "I can't have it so! I've learned to love you like a mother."

"Thanks, Mr. Forrest," she whispered. "I'm so glad to hear you say so! But the clock is running down."

"Only two weeks gone," he cried. "I didn't think of this."

"But," she whispered again, "it is all right. I have done what I could. It was such a comfort to see how glad and grateful they were! I couldn't desert them.

"And," she added, "I haven't any fear. It's as well now as ever. It must come; and it had better come in the way of duty. Life purchased by neglect of the suffering isn't worth having" — and her voice sunk away.

"But speak to me once more," he cried. "Is it all well?"

"All well," she added, rousing for a moment. "If, as I hope, there's a future, we'll meet. If not, still God does us no wrong. We've had life, — a chance to help our fellow-men. Be true, and — all is — well."

And she sunk into a lethargy, from which she roused no more. Mr. Forrest put his cheek to her lips to find if he could feel her breath; and, seeing that she breathed no more, he kissed her forehead, and sprinkled it with tears.

"O God!" he exclaimed, "whatever she is called, here sleeps one of thine own saints."

The town was full of grief, and loud were her praises on the lips of all the common people, when they heard that she had given up her life for them; and for a time all criticism of her opinions was shamed into silence in the presence of her noble life and nobler death.

As her house was small, and so many of those she had

befriended clamored for the privilege of following her to the grave, it was determined that the funeral should be in the church. Under ordinary circumstances it would have been opposed as a profanation of the sanctuary; but any such move now would have been so frowned upon by the public sentiment, that it was not to be thought of.

So the very next afternoon the church was crowded with a sorrowing throng. As Mr. Forrest looked over them he could not help thinking of the story of Dorcas, and how, when she was dead, the widows came together weeping, and showing the garments that Dorcas had made; and, indeed, he read this story as a part of the scripture-service appropriate to the scene.

When a hymn had been sung, he rose, and gave out his text, —

"I have fought a good fight, I have finished my course, I have kept the faith: henceforth there is laid up for me the crown which the Lord, the righteous judge, shall give me at that day."

After his long struggles and her motherly friendship, and this heroic sacrifice of herself, he was in no mood to pay regard to theological prejudices. He must speak his heart out, if he spoke at all.

He began with a brief sketch of her life, as she had given it to him in their many conversations. He pictured her hard, puritanical childhood; how she had longed for fatherly and motherly kisses and love, when only severe care and the hard training of duty had been accorded her; how she had been repressed and discouraged to keep back, as they thought, any sinful pride. He spoke of restricted Sundays, and how church and religion had been made hateful to her by showing her only its angular side ; how even her love for birds and flowers was repressed and denied, as savoring of idle vanity ; then, how she had fought her way out of this into a belief in and love for a God who was the tender, loving Father of us all. He spoke of her married life, of her devotion and sacrifice to her husband ; and then, amid the broken sobs of the many she had helped, he pictured her life of beneficence in Bluffton. And when he reached the last two weeks, and what she had dared and borne for others, and with no thought of or hope for reward, his own voice faltered, and he could hardly command his words.

Pausing then a moment, he said, —

"Such, friends, is her past life, and such her death. I well know the odium that attaches to her in this city on account of her theological opinions. But to me it seems paltry, in the presence of her high and holy sacrifice, to speak of such superficial distinctions. If ye cannot gather grapes of thorns, nor figs of thistles, as the Master says, then by what name shall we call her? Grapes and figs of noble character and unselfish service for her fellows she most assuredly has borne. And, since the tree is known by its fruits, she can have been none other than sound-hearted and true. I dare to call hers a noble Christian life. Let those criticise her who have lived as well. And, if none others lift their voices, there will be the silence of reverent praise.

"She has fought a good fight,— a fight for all good and

noble causes. She has kept the faith,— a faith in God, in
duty, in mankind. She has finished her course, — a course
back over which she can look, and see no cause for shame.
And now, I trust, there is indeed kept for her a crown ;
for the Lord, being a righteous judge, must love and reward
righteousness in his children.

"It seems almost an insult, in the presence of her pure
spirit, to defend her. But, if 'in all nations he who doeth
the will of God is accepted of him,' then surely there will
be welcome for her. What she has thought is little : what
she has done is much. The creed is little if it do not make
the deed. And, when the deed is found, the creed may be
inferred. And if indeed there be a heaven where righteous
souls are after death, then at her coming there must have
risen the cry, 'Lift up your heads, O ye gates,' that the righteous one may enter in ! "

He then closed his simple service by reading the following verses : —

> ✗ "O apple, apple, on the bough, ✗
>   What of your root ? " cried he :
> " Thou lookest sweet and very fair ;
>   But tell me about the tree."
>
> The apple replied, "Come, taste the fruit :
>   Thou need'st not dig about
> The root, nor saw the trunk in two,
>   To find its nature out.
>
> If I be sound in core, and sweet,
>   Then trust the tree and root ;
> For the juices of the tree do make
>   The flavor of the fruit.

If the fruit is bitter, no matter then
How fair the trunk may be ;
It cumbers the ground : so take thine axe,
And, gardener, hew down the tree."

So is it in the lives of men :
The fair outside may show
Like a tree of paradise ; but God
If it bear good fruit doth know.

The procession formed, after the great multitude had taken their last look, and wound its slow way round the bluff to the hillside cemetery as it sloped down to the river. The grave had been opened beside her husband ; and the loving thought of the poor, who could pay her no other tribute, had covered all the freshly thrown-out clods with evergreens, and with the same material had completely lined the grave. So as the coffin was lowered it seemed to be let down into an amaranthine bower of fadeless green. The repulsiveness of the grave was gone ; and she was only put away to sleep on the green bed of the branches.

The scene was one of wondrous though saddening beauty. The sun was low in the west, and his sloping beams fell through and slipped under the trees, and lay like golden bars upon the green of the grass. The ripples on the river twinkled and sparkled in the light, and stretched off, crinkling and shimmering by the islands, till lost as the headlands closed in. The air was soft and still, hardly moving a leaf, save where now and then a silver poplar kept up its perpetual aspen tremble. And, as Mr. Forrest read the last words

of the service, it seemed to him he could ask no more
fitting or sunny close to a life in whose sky had been so
much of cloud and storm. When he had pronounced the
benediction, he murmured under his breath, —

"'So He giveth his beloved sleep.'"

And now when the formal ceremony was over, they gathered about him, this one and that, to tell him of some little
deed of mercy of which he had never heard before.

When all else had gone, Mr. Forrest staid beside the
old sexton, who was filling in the grave. He lived in a little
cottage near the cemetery-gate, a mile or more from the
town. He stopped in the midst of his work, leaning on his
spade ; and, when he had wiped his eyes with his rough
sleeve, he said, —

"O Mr. Forrest, I didn't think she'd come so soon arter
I'd put my own little one in the ground ! "

"Have you, then, lost a child lately?"

"Yes, sir : little Clary's gone since you been away. Mrs.
Grey heard we's sick, and come clear up the hill here to
help us, though she's all wore out then. We're too poor to
have a doctor ; and, 'sides, the doctors was too driven down
to the city. An' then, when she died there warn't no minister
't I felt I could ask, because I don't go nowhere to church.
An' this blessed angel, she come up an' put her little white
dress on Clary, and put a rose in her hand ; an' then," —
here he choked a minute, and buried his face in his hands,
— "I couldn't 'ford no hearse : so we two, and mother all
broke down, an' leadin' Johnny and Fred, we took the little
white pine coffin on my old wheel-barrow ; and she helped

me put her away to sleep over under that little tree in the corner. God bless her ! she was like the sunshine, ready to look down soft and sweet on all on us."

And here he sat down on the heap of earth, and sobbed like a child.

XV.

MADGE ENTREATS.

ONLY a few days had passed before Mr. Forrest learned
that the words he had spoken of Mrs. Grey were to
come back to trouble him.   His breath had started a breeze
that might gather to a storm.   At first, in the excitement
and fresh sorrow of her loss, the unchurched reverence for
her was a sentiment too strong to be overlooked.   But all
these sorrows pass away, and people become absorbed in
their own life again.   Then his words were remembered;
and the orthodox party in all the churches took the alarm.
A minister of the gospel had dared to set up as a pattern-
saint, and even profanely open the gates of heaven to, an
"infidel."   It was not to be endured.   Those who had kept
at a safe distance when the cholera was abroad now came
out boldly to depreciate the services of her who had given
her life for those in danger.   Her devotion counted for
little : her opinions only were remembered.   "He that
believeth and is baptized shall be saved; and he that believeth not shall be damned," said the Baptists.   Each
different church thought her soul was certainly lost, because
she was not "of them."   For very few of the people in

Bluffton had any hope of the salvation of members of other churches even, except their own. So of course there was small hope for one not in any church at all.

Mr. Smiley made a special visitation of the parish, and, in the claimed interests of the church, prayed and wept with all the old ladies over their pastor's heresy. He said, —

"Why, only think what it means! If Mrs. Grey is to be sent right to heaven, what need is there of our blessed gospel of salvation? Where is salvation by faith? What is the use of prayer and revival meetings? Why send the gospel to the heathen? The other churches all about us are pointing their fingers at us, and wondering that we allow such things to go on."

And when he met Mr. Forrest, coming out of a house after one of these visits, he smiled the same sweet smile as ever, — the one he ordinarily *wore*, — and grasped his hand with a —

"I'm so glad, my dear pastor, that you were away during this fearful divine visitation! We did what we could; but the will of God will take its way. Mrs. Grey will be a great loss to the poor. A woman of great benevolence was Mrs. Grey. Only it is a pity she had not the grace of God in her heart."

Mr. Forrest had to bite his lips to keep back a sharp retort on his cant, that now he had learned to estimate; but, crowding back his words, he turned abruptly, and walked away.

And now the town was beginning to whisper under its breath something more appetizing to its vulgar taste, if not

so great a theological crime as heresy. Rumor, particularly
if scandalous, seems to have been in league with Puck, and
to have learned from him how to "put a girdle round the
earth in forty minutes."

Mr. Forrest had hardly been back from New York a day
before Mr. Smiley heard that at which he appeared to be
unspeakably shocked; though in reality he caught at it, as
something that would help him in his opposition to the minister. This opposition was by this time well known to Mr.
Forrest, though it had been kept carefully masked. So far
as he could learn, it dated from the first, and had no other
motive than the instinctive dislike of a man to hearing perpetually recommended that which he had the least of, viz.,
character.

"Deacon," said Mr. Smiley, addressing Deacon Putney, as
they met on the sidewalk, "just come up in my office a
minute."

And when seated, he said,—

"I didn't want to speak of it on the street, for fear somebody should overhear; but it is my painful duty to inform
you that the purity and honor of our Zion are threatened."

It was always his "painful duty" to say those things that
he knew were going to hurt; but no man living was ever
more ready to perform "painful duties" of this kind.

"Why, Mr. Smiley," said the deacon, his dull eyes kind-
ling with curiosity, "what *do* you mean?"

"Haven't you heard it?" He knew he hadn't, but he
wanted to make it appear as though any one might have told
him.

"Why, no : I haven't heard any thing."

"Well, I'm so thankful. I feared it might have got out; and I am so anxious to spare the church!"

In reality he was "so anxious" to have the privilege of first telling it, and appearing to be anxious for the "good of the cause."

"But what is it?" anxiously inquired the deacon.

"Oh! I can't bear to speak of it: only the officers of the church, the 'watchmen that stand on the towers of Zion,' and whose duty it is to warn the people, ought to know. But who would have thought it? He seemed so upright, if he wasn't orthodox."

"Well, do tell me what it is!" burst out the deacon, who was getting very impatient.

Then Mr. Smiley laid his hand on the deacon's knee, and, leaning forward and looking him in the face, said in a low and awe-ful whisper, —

"Why, I've just got it from good authority, that Mr. Forrest, when in New York, was seen to go, with another man, to a house of notorious reputation."

"You — don't — say!" slowly and emphatically exclaimed the deacon.

"And that isn't all, nor the worst," continued Mr. Smiley; "for he took a woman from this very house, and brought her on the cars all the way West with him; and she is now concealed somewhere in Maple City. And, though he has been home but a few days, he has already been up there once to see her. Where will such things end?"

And when they had talked it over in all its bearings, and

agreed that it ought to be kept quiet, they went out, and whispered it all over the town.

But Mr. Forrest neither knew nor cared for any of these things. He was not anxious as to what Bluffton thought of him now; for he had a sorer trial in the state of mind of Miss Hartley.

It was a rainy spring afternoon, when, having spent his morning in his study, and the weather making it impossible for him to do out-door work, he thought he would spend an hour or two with Madge.

Judge Hartley had heard the whispered scandal; but he was just enough not to believe all he heard, and he would not trouble his daughter with such things until it became necessary. So neither Miss Hartley nor Mr. Forrest knew the underground gossip of the town. But the judge and many others had talked to her about his theological heresies. She had as yet too much faith in him to think that he could be seriously out of the way. Still the increase of criticism since the funeral of Mrs. Grey determined her to have a talk with him.

"Mark," said she, as they sat together in her chamber, and watched and listened to the rain on the window, "do you know there is one thing that is beginning to trouble me very much?"

"Why, what is it, Madge? Nothing ought to trouble one I love so much; and it shall not, if in my power to prevent it."

"It makes me glad to hear you speak like that; for you are just the one that can prevent it."

"Well, tell me what it is that I can do."

"You can be like other ministers, Mark. I can't bear to hear you talked about so."

"What do they say?"

"They say you are drifting away from the truth. Tell me, are you?"

"O Madge! you've touched the one sore spot of my life. Yes, Madge, I suppose I am drifting, or sailing, away from what many think is the truth."

"You will help me, then, by coming back?"

"I fear you've asked me the one thing that is out of my power. One cannot believe at will."

"But, dear Mark, why can't you preach as other ministers do?"

"Would you respect me if I preached what I do not believe?"

"Why, no, of course I could not; but why can't you believe?"

"Because I have thought and read and studied."

"But why need you read and study the books that upset your faith? They can't be any good books that do that."

"I believe them to be wise and good books, Madge."

"But you are young, Mark. May you not be mistaken? The Church that has believed these things so long, the great majority of learned men, they all must be right. They can't be mistaken."

"The truth doesn't go by majorities, Madge: Christianity was once in the minority."

"Of course; but that came by inspiration. But it has been settled so long, it must be true."

"But even the majority of learned men are not orthodox."

"I know, the great numbers of scientific men and philosophers : they follow their own wisdom, and get led astray. But father thinks it is wilful blindness on their part."

"Well, Madge, it almost kills me to have to give you pain."

"But you don't have to give me pain, Mark. You have only to be like other men in this matter. Why can't you at least let these disputed questions alone, and only preach the simple gospel ? "

"These problems haunt me. And then, all these questions are linked together. I can't treat one, and let the rest alone. I sometimes think I shall have to leave the church."

"O Mark ! don't talk that way unless you want to break my heart. It would kill father to have me follow you out of the church. And I couldn't leave him in his old age, and have him think me lost. His dear old face would haunt me forever. I don't know much about these great questions. I only know I love you, I trust you. But oh, isn't there some way that you can let these things rest ? "

"But, dear Madge " —

"Oh, don't say there isn't ! " she broke in passionately. "If you love me, I entreat you, dear Mark, don't think and study these horrible things. It frightens me, Mark. May it not be that Satan is tempting you, and leading you astray? Father says he often comes in the guise of human wisdom, to lead men away from the simplicity of the gospel."

"There, Madge," he cried, "please don't talk so any more. I'll try : for your sake I'll try to do any and all things save such as you would despise me for doing."

"Do find some way," she added. "I can't abandon father. And yet I fear it would kill me to stay with him, and lose you. I'm only a weak woman, Mark. I only know I love you dearly. I am not wise enough to help your thinking. You must settle that. I suppose, if father did not hold me by cords of duty as well as love, I should believe any thing you told me was true. But O Mark, don't leave me, don't leave me ! "

And she flung herself into his waiting arms, and poured out her trouble and anxiety in weeping.

Mark soothed and comforted her as well as he knew how ; but did not tell her of the horrible fear, that weighed down his heart, that this was not the first nor worst of their sorrow.

In his study that evening, when the night outside was dark as the rayless heaven of his soul, he went over again his lonely struggle. It was no longer a question as to whether he was to be true to his own soul ; and he was too clear-headed not to see that he must be prepared to face the worst. So his battle was only a desperate struggle with the inevitable.

He plainly saw that leaving Bluffton and orthodoxy was separation from Madge. Not that she did not love him enough to follow him to the world's end. He knew she did. But he knew also that she loved her father not only, but that she felt bound to him in this matter by the whole strength of her moral nature. He would think her lost to God and him forever ; and she could not " bring down his gray hairs with sorrow to the grave." Even could he have

persuaded her to break this bond of her moral nature, that
linked her to her childhood and her father so firmly, he
would not have dared to do it. It was just this moral force
of character in her, that made the tenderness of her womanhood so lovely. He could not pluck his flower with such
violence as to strip it of its petals.

"O God!" he cried, " could I not have been spared this?
Must love, too, be sacrificed? I could give all else gladly;
but this is more than I can bear!"

He walked his study in silence, and alone with his sorrow.
And, as he walked and thought, he took from his pocket-
book a scrap that he had cut from a newspaper, and read
over again some verses in which he had found an echo of
his own sadness. He had looked at them often of late, and
he saw himself between the lines.

THE LONE VOYAGER.

'Twas ever so, that he who dared
    To sail upon a sea unknown
Must go upon a voyage unshared,
    And brave its perils all alone.

Columbus, with his faith alone,
    Sailed for new worlds beyond the sea;
Trusted behind by few or none, —
    Around him faithless mutiny.

And he who, not content to sit
    And dream upon the shores of truth,
Watching the sea-bird fancies flit,
    And wavelets creep, through all his youth, —

Must sail unblest of those behind,
   While love turns to reproach her tone:
The loving God alone is kind
   To him who dares to sail alone.

"But is even God kind?" he exclaimed. "I cry, but he does not answer. O truth, truth! wilt thou strip thy votaries of all, — leaving them only their weary search for thee?"

XVI.

A TERRIBLE SUSPICION.

IN small towns the store is to the men what the sewing-circle is to the women, their intellectual and gossip exchange; and the staple conversation is commonly no whit more important or dignified in the one place than it is in the other.

Deacon Putney's hardware store was the favorite place of resort. From the nature of the trade, the men could sit and smoke, and were not likely to be interrupted. The deacon himself was always much readier to talk than to work; so he left his not overcrowded custom to his clerks, while he sat in a basket-work armchair by the stove, and assisted in settling the last question of public moment.

The question naturally uppermost now was the new scandal about the minister. If you saw two or three people stopping together on a street-corner, you were safe in supposing that this was the theme of their conversation. If Mr. Forrest came by, they spoke of something else, gave him a pleasant greeting, and then, as he passed, some one would remark, —

"Nobody 'd 'a' thought it, would they? Just look at him. Fine-looking man. Pity!"

And then they would go on speculating about it again.

About this time aunt Sally Rawson "felt it to be her duty" to speak to Miss Hartley on the subject. Some one always "feels bound" to tell what is none of his or her business to just the wrong person. So she put on her bonnet and striped shawl, and started up to the judge's.

"Miss Hartley," said she, "air you aware what a name Mr. Forrest is gittin' 'bout town?"

"What do you mean?" said she with some severity; for, whatever had happened, she felt it no business of an outsider to speak, so long as her father kept silence.

"Well, 'f you're goin' to git your back up when one means to do you a service, then no matter."

"What have you to say?"

"Well, I thought 't you'd ought to know that Mr. Forrest was seen with a woman in sarcumstances where 't didn't look jest right, an'"—

"Mrs. Rawson, you can leave the house, if you please," said she quietly. "I can learn all I wish to know of Mr. Forrest, from those who have a better right to speak to me on the subject."

And aunt Sally flounced out of the house in a rage. She went straight over to Mrs. Buck, and exclaimed,—

"Well, if Miss Hartley ain't the sauciest, stuck-up-est, pert body I ever see!"

And then they guessed that any "gal" that would act that way "warn't no better'n she should be, herself." She "was goin'," aunt Sally said, "to do her a favor;" but she "guessed she'd wait one while 'fore she offered to do another."

Meantime Miss Hartley had such faith in Mr. Forrest, and in her father too, that she did not even care to question as to what aunt Sally was hinting at.

It was only natural that the smouldering material should flame out at the store. Here, then, let us go and listen, and see into what voices it will hiss.

"It's only natural, I say," said Clem. Haydon: "when a man gets loose in doctrine, then look out to see him loose in morals next. You know I told you so when he first come."

Clem. Haydon, so called familiarly after the Western fashion, was a middle-aged man, and an elder in the United Presbyterian church. He looked upon the Congregational church as lacking in soundness, anyway. And while very zealous for the kingdom of God, like many others, he was not over-sorry to see any other than the United Presbyterian branch going down.

Deacon Putney had learned from the majority opinion of those immediately about him, that Mr. Forrest was not sound; and yet he did not enjoy having a member of a rival church get any handle against his own. So he replied with a bit of vinegar in his tone, —

"P'raps your memory's better'n mine. I disremember your ever saying any thing about it when he first come."

"But I did, though, right here in this store. I saw well enough 'twas comin'."

"Some folks' hind-sight's a heap better'n their foresight," observed uncle Zeke sarcastically. "I don't 'low you seen it comin'; for I don't believe ther's nothin' come, nohow, 'cept a lot o' mare's-nests you fellers 's a-settin' on."

"Oh! he means well," patronizingly observed Mr. Smiley, "but of course he don't know what we know. And then what does he know about the doctrines of the gospel that Mr. Forrest slights?"

"Waal, I d' know, and I don't care much 'bout yer doctrines o' the gospel. But Mr. Forrest preaches the *practice* of the gospel a blamed sight better'n you foller him, anyhow."

"Oh, yes! you think so," sneered Mr. Smiley. "His trip to New York was nice practice of the gospel, wasn't it?"

"All I got ter say is," responded uncle Zeke, "that, till folks shows their evidence, to be talkin' round and blackenin' folks' characters looks a big sight to me like breakin' one o' the c'mandments anyway. Ain't there suthin' in ther' bout 'bearin' false witness'?"

"Well hit for you, uncle Zeke," broke in Judge Harrington, a rough-spoken but ardent admirer of Mr. Forrest. 'You all know I don't go much on your churches anyhow; but I do like an honest man. I don't care about your fights over doctrine, and I haven't been to church for five years before Mr. Forrest came. I understand he's suffering now because we outsiders like him. But do you want to know why I go to hear him? Because there isn't another —— minister in town that dares to preach out what he believes. You make liars of them anyhow. You stand them up in your pulpits, and then say to them, 'Don't you dare to find out and tell us any thing we don't already know, or, snap! goes the bread and butter out of your mouths.' I wonder they ain't a bigger set of pudding-heads than the most of them already are."

"I can't countenance such language by my presence," said Mr. Smiley, and pompously withdrew.

"I don't wonder," said uncle Zeke with an air of dry humor: "do you know, I never saw a man what seemed to be so lonesome-like round where three or four fellers was tellin' the truth."

"Well," said Clem. Haydon, who, from prudence or from some other reason, didn't see fit to pick up uncle Zeke's remark, "there isn't any other foundation for a pure morality but faith in the Bible and the Church; and whatever else Mr. Forrest has done, or has not, he has undermined respect for these."

"But," replied Judge Harrington, who, though rough, was a good lawyer and a man well read in history, "perhaps, if that is so, you will be kind enough to explain how it happens that the historical 'ages of faith,' when nobody dared to doubt either Bible or Church, were the most completely immoral ages of Christendom."

Knowing his business and his "confession of faith," he could only reply, —

"I don't believe they were. My minister would know it if it was so."

"But," responded the judge, "just as I told you, he wouldn't dare say it, if he did know it. If he did, you'd 'send him in his resignation,' as black Jim said the other day about their minister. And he knows it mighty well."

"But doesn't morality rest on the Bible?" he feebly protested.

"No," said the judge. "Nations that never heard of

your Bible are a big sight more moral than many of the church-members in town. Morality and religion made the Bible in the first place; though religion had more to do with some parts of it than morality did."

"Well, I do' know," said Deacon Putney: "*I* think if there weren't no Bible and no Devil, there wouldn't be much goodness."

"When people behave because they're afraid of the Devil, do you want to know what I think of 'em?" inquired the judge. He expected no reply, and so continued, "I think they're sneaks and cowards instead of Christians. Mr. Forrest preaches the best rules and principles of right living I ever heard in Bluffton; and I have my opinion — which isn't a very high one — of the people that are trying to undermine him."

By this time the judge and Uncle Zeke had withdrawn. Clem. Haydon and the Deacon and one or two more of their kind now had it all to themselves. Knowing about what they would say, it is hardly worth our while to listen longer.

XVII.

AN EXCHANGE AT MAPLE CITY.

ON the next Sunday Mr. Forrest was to be at Maple
City on exchange with the minister there.

On the Friday preceding, Mr. Smiley called a meeting
of personal sympathizers at his office. Here they canvassed
the condition of affairs; and Mr. Forrest was officially noti-
fied, that, at the church-meeting that evening, steps would
be taken to call a council of the neighboring churches to
pass upon the matter of his doctrinal soundness. "Letters-
missive" would be sent out Saturday; the churches could
appoint delegates on Sunday; and the council was to meet
on the following Thursday.

Mr. Forrest was not at all surprised; for he supposed it
would come soon. He did not care to stand the trial, for
his own part; but ministerial friends, with whom he had
discussed the coming possibility, urged him to stand for
their sakes. They preached similar doctrine themselves;
and they wanted the matter brought to a test, as to whether
there was any freedom in the church.

Though his sympathies were all with Mr. Smiley's party,
yet Judge Hartley took but little active part in the matter;

for he saw how distressed it made his daughter. It was indeed a sad blow to her; for she saw Mark branded, and cast out of the church, in her foreboding fancy; and that meant torn from her, or breaking her father's heart. She had always been his pet; and now in his old age he leaned upon her. So she plead with Mr. Forrest, whenever she saw him now, until he hardly dared to meet her, lest her sorrow and his own love should persuade him to warp or twist the truth from its straight uprightness.

By this time Mr. Forrest was well aware of the whispers concerning his character about town; and yet he kept perfectly still, and made no explanation. He had no doubt these rumors would complicate affairs at the council, and yet he kept still. He only hoped Madge had heard nothing that might add a new pang to her sorrow; but he dared not ask her, lest his question should be a revelation of what he hoped she did not know.

Sunday came, and with it the opportunity Mr. Forrest wanted to talk affairs over with Tom. Of course he stopped at his house. After dinner was over, they had the long afternoon to themselves. The house faced the street; and a long piazza ran round three sides, — the two ends and the rear. Vines clambered over it; and through their leafy arches one looked out on a scene of wondrous loveliness. The sloping river-bank, covered with native trees, stretched away, and by natural terraces reached the water, which here and there glistened between the branches. The ground was laid out in lawn and flower-bed, with now and then an artificial lake or fountain. The whole was ornamented with casts of statuary, or piles of shell, or stone covered with lichen and moss.

Here, then, in the warm May afternoon, the two friends sat, tilted back in their chairs, and with their feet on the rail about the piazza, as men always love to sit to rest and talk. Tom smoked his pipe on such occasions, and with the clouds of smoke filled in the pauses of their conversation; and, though he did not care for it alone, Mark would then take a cigar, and keep him company.

They had talked for a few minutes, when Tom took out his pipe, and said, —

"What did she say when you talked with her this morning, Mark? Isn't she ready for you to speak yet?"

"No, Tom: she can't bring her mind to it; and I don't much wonder, after all that has passed."

"But it's a mighty pity, old boy, for you to submit to have the puppies wagging their tongues about you all over Bluffton, when a word would end it."

"No matter: I can stand it. I promised her in New York that she should take her own time to speak; and she shall, at whatever cost to me."

"But if she only knew" —

"But she shall not know, Tom. She shall not risk every thing now for the sake of saving me a little inconvenience."

"It will make things hot for you at the council."

"Then let it be hot. She shall know that I did for her every thing I could."

"Then you won't speak anyhow, even then?"

"No, of course not. And you must not, either. You know you've promised me."

"Yes, I know I have; but I wish I had not." He thought a little, and added, —

"It was a foolish promise. She might as well speak now as any time."

"She shall wait till she's forty, if she chooses, Tom."

"But what of Madge? Does she know?"

"I hope not. But, if she does, *she* has sense, if the rest haven't. That's the smallest of my troubles about her."

"Women are jealous and suspicious, Mark. You mustn't ask too much of them."

"If she can't trust me a little now, I'd like to find it out."

"Well, you'll have your own way, I suppose."

"But, Tom, look here. To change the subject," said Mark, "I've noticed, ever since I've been in Bluffton, that my intimacy with you has been a crime in the eyes of Smiley. Beside your heresy, has he any special reason for disliking you?"

"The same reason that all shams have for disliking the man that finds them out. I know him too well: that's all."

"Have you ever had business transactions with him?"

"I should think I had. Having paid a tolerably high price for the recollection, I don't think I'll forget it soon either."

"He makes a good impression on one at first."

"Yes: he's one of your devil-an-angel-of-light kind of fellows. That smile of his, and his pious tone, have a commercial value, Mark, and he always wears them."

"I don't see how a man can assume to be what he isn't."

"Why, his face has got to have some sort of look on it,

you know; and it don't cost any more to have a holy one than any other."

"He has always appeared friendly to me, Tom."

"Of course: why not? Appearing friendly isn't much trouble."

"But what have I done to offend him? I hardly understand it. He hasn't so gigantic an intellect but that I can claim, without immodesty, to satisfy him that way."

"That's good, Mark. I'm almost afraid you're simple. His instincts are sound. He feels, from the first, that he has no standing on the basis of the kind of gospel you preach. He's got to be saved by emotion and an external atonement, or there's no show for him. You preach character all the time, and he don't like it; for, don't you see, you're 'bulling' the market on just that commodity that he happens to be out of. Unless he can 'bear' you on that line, he's bankrupt."

"But, Tom, do you think he means to be dishonest? or does he cheat himself as well as others?"

"I hardly know: he's a puzzle to me."

"I've noticed," continued Mark, "that sometimes a man gets into ways of doing business where he's hard and dishonest so long as the effects are remote, and don't touch his feeling by an actual sight of the results; and at the same time he's tender and kind in cases of actual want about him."

"Yes, I know: conscience is a queer thing. He seems to have his conscience under as thorough control as his face: it will smile on any thing he wants it to."

"Now, as touching this matter, no man would willingly tell things to his own discredit.   But he has himself told me of transactions of his that were simply outrageous; and he seemed to be perfectly unconscious of there being any thing about them but smartness."

"I know: conscience seems to get rusty, like old scales, — don't indicate the weight accurately."

"And yet, again, I occasionally find myself compelled to think that he purposely goes wrong.   He seems deliberately to choose his way.   Now, not long ago he told me frankly that even if I was right and he wrong on doctrinal matters, he didn't want to know it; for he didn't propose to change — 'choosing darkness rather than light.'"

"Of course he doesn't.   His business character is simply rotten.   His 'scheme of salvation' still gives him a chance. Yours doesn't: don't you see?"

"But what do you *know* about his business, Tom?"

"Well, several things.   And I've paid a good price for my knowledge.   For instance, I owned a share in a silver-mine in Colorado.   It was a stock-company.   I had been out and inspected it, found it all right, and was going to buy more shares.   He also found out its value.   Then, by secret agents, he got in his hands enough of the stock to control it, and then turned the water into it, filled it full, and let it stand.   The rest of us, being in a minority, could do nothing.   He 'froze us all out,' as it is called; i.e., made the mine so valueless that stock was worth nothing, and the owners had to sell for a song.   I could stand it; but it ruined some who had invested there all they had.   After he got —

that is, *stole* — all the other stock, then he turned to, cleared
the mine, and made a pile out of it.

"That's the kind of money he helps on the Lord's cause
with."

"Does he do such things often?"

"No oftener than he gets a chance. He's always honest
when he can't help it. I happen to know that he is in the
habit of 'doctoring' his accounts and books so as to make
them look all right to the men whose money he is using; and
then suddenly, through a mysterious dispensation of Providence, he will fail. And then he is able to get a new carriage and a span."

"It doesn't seem possible that a man can live like that."

"But facts 'lay over' possibilities. Take another little
transaction. I owned a piece of ground that he wanted.
I also wanted it, and so refused to sell. He went and
hunted up all the old titles from the first, and found somewhere, forty or fifty years back, a legal flaw, of which I
knew nothing, and that in equity of course did not
touch my right of possession. Then he comes and
says, 'You can sell at my price, or I'll take it away from
you.' I was helpless, and had to submit. Now, it isn't any
particular wonder that a man whose 'best holt,' as they say,
is piety, should look with slight disfavor on a man who
knows such things about him."

"Well, I should think not."

"I must give you just one more taste of his righteousness. Not long since, through the failure of a man he was
dealing with, about three hundred barrels of flour came into

his hands. It was of the very poorest quality, made of damaged wheat. While it lay in the storehouse, he sent a man to remove all the brands, and with a little fresh paint transformed the whole lot into the finest quality of St. Louis flour, making, by a simple mark on the head, a difference of some three or four dollars a barrel.

"But the best of it was afterward. The next Sunday he addressed the Sunday school on the cross of Christ, and mingled his tears with theirs over his own pathos. And at the close, he told them that since the Lord had been singularly kind to him during the past week, and had specially blessed his humble efforts to make money for His own cause, he would therefore make them a present of a new library, — the old one to be sent to some other needy school; and he also had some pictures and mottoes hung up about the room, the two most conspicuous of them being, 'Honesty is the best policy,' and 'Virtue is its own reward.'

"Oh, but he's a model ! "

"Well, Tom, no wonder he dislikes you."

"But," said he with an ironical tone, " it's only my 'infidelity' he dislikes."

"You know, Tom," said Mark, changing the subject with the air of one who had got all of that he wanted, " that Smiley had a sister; did you not? "

"Yes: I know a good deal about her, but I never saw her."

"Well, what do you know about her? I have my reasons for wishing to know."

"I know this: All the family is dead except Smiley and this one sister, Mary. She was the youngest child, and must be about nineteen or twenty, I should guess. I have heard she was frail, apparently timid, and yet has a will of her own."

"Has Smiley been kind to her?"

"Yes, before people. But he is her legal guardian; and the father, a hard old man, left her share of the property in Smiley's hands, so that she comes into it only on condition that she marries to suit him. The old gentleman thought women and girls should never be trusted, but ought to obey the father or brothers; and Smiley was his pet, a boy after his own heart. So the story runs. And indeed, when I first met Smiley, he pretended confidences, and told me much of it himself."

"But she hasn't been in Bluffton since I came West."

"No: she lives a part of the time East; has been at school, and visiting with friends. So of course you haven't seen her either."

"I am quite familiar with her face," said Mark equivocally. And he added, "I have often seen her photograph, so I should know her anywhere. She is quite a favorite in Bluffton; and, indeed, Madge has taken a great fancy to her. So I almost feel as if I knew her."

"But do you know Smiley's latest persecution of her?"

"About her engagement?"

"Yes."

"I have heard something. What is it?" For Mark wished to know if it corresponded with what he had heard from another source.

"Well, she became engaged, without consulting the high and mighty Smiley, to a capital fellow from Denver City. His crime was, that he had his fortune still to make, though he was in a fair way to make it. Smiley himself had fixed it up, that she was to marry one of his partners in a big speculation, so that he could get a bigger finger in the affair through family influence. For his sister, like every thing and everybody else, is only to him so much available means in the money market."

"Yes, that sounds like what she told me," mused Mark, without thinking what he was saying.

"*She* told you : who told you?" quickly inquired Tom.

Mark saw that he had almost let slip his secret prematurely ; but he rallied, and replied, —

"Oh, a lady friend I met in New York ! She seemed to know all about it, and we talked it over together."

"Oh, yes !" said Tom : "your answer was so queer that it startled me a bit."

Mark did not choose to explain, and so continued, —

"But do you know what is to come of it ? "

"Only that she rushed East suddenly a year ago, just before you came, to escape Smiley's persecutions, and said she'd die before she'd marry at anybody's dictation. And a strange rumor is afloat within the last month, that she disappeared suddenly from her friends in Boston, and Smiley has been writing everywhere to get on the track of her. I reckon he doesn't care much, only for the 'honor' of his family. He'll do almost any thing to save the family reputation. He'd even let her marry her own choice, I think, if public opinion touched his pride in the matter."

"Good! I'm glad to hear you say that, Tom; for perhaps his pride will help me through the matter."

"Help you through what matter? You're talking riddles now. What have you got to do about it anyway?"

"Perhaps more than you know. She didn't want me to let you know, if I could help it."

"Well, what are you talking about, Mark?"

"You said a little while ago, that you had never seen Miss Smiley."

"Of course I said so; for I haven't."

"Yes, you have, Tom; for she dined with us to-day."

"Good heavens! you don't mean it! This beautiful young woman you brought from New York" —

"Is Smiley's sister, Tom. There, it's out now."

"Well, this is dramatic enough. Why in creation didn't you tell me so before?"

"It was her wish that I shouldn't, and you are not to know her even now. I told you because I thought perhaps you might help me work on Smiley so as to save her."

"But this is stranger than what usually goes for fiction. If it was Smiley himself, I don't think I should be over-anxious to save him. But, by Jove, I do pity the girl; and I'm with you to the extent of any thing I can do."

"And yet, remember, I've promised her not to reveal her till she consents. She's evidently afraid of her brother, and thinks he will cast her off."

"Let him cast, if he will. I know the man she's engaged to, and he's a generous, noble fellow. When he knows her story, he's a different man from what I think him, if he doesn't take her to his heart.   Her suffering, and even the touch of sin, — if there is any, — was all for his sake ; and he's a villain if he deserts her."

"I'm glad to hear you say that of him, for it looks like a streak of daylight.   If men were only a little more sensible, there'd be less ruin in the world."

XVIII.

THE COUNCIL.

THURSDAY came, and with it the gathering of ministers and delegates from all the Bluffton association.
The town was excited. It was usually dull; for only the
commoner class of peripatetic amusements and theatrical
troupes ever visited the place; and these did not furnish
entertainment for the church-members, because they never
attended such things — except when they were away from
home. Perhaps it would be unjust to say that hundreds
of people were glad there was going to be a trial; and yet,
since there *was* going to be a trial, hundreds were glad they
could go. Perhaps people do not like to have their neighbors houses burn up; but, if they are going to burn, they do
like to see the fire. So everybody prepared to be present,
and see the permitted entertainment that was going to
be exhibited free.

Mr. Forrest had had a most painful meeting and parting
with Madge. He knew by her face that the night had
been spent in weeping more than in sleep. But now she
was calm with the calmness of one prepared in prison for
the inevitable execution. It was not Mark only, who was

to be tried: her own destiny was to be passed upon; and already she saw herself alone, with all she had learned to look upon as fairest and sweetest in the future, blasted and turned to a desolation.

They sat together a half-hour in silence, brooding over their own thoughts. Then the tears started in Madge's eyes, and she cried, —

"O Mark, Mark! Is there no way out of it even yet?"

"I can only take the next step that is clear, dear Madge; and what will follow, God only knows."

And now for a moment she lost control of herself, and, out of the anguish of her love, entreated, plead, and almost upbraided him, as though he had willingly brought it upon them. Then she begged his forgiveness, and said, —

"I don't know what I say. I'm cruel: as though it were not hard for you, as well as for me!"

He comforted her as best he could, and then they parted. Once more he was to see her, and then — what then, he dared not allow himself to think.

The hour for the council was called. The church was full. The moderator and scribe were chosen, and they were ready for business.

On behalf of the church, Mr. Smiley had been chosen to present the charges against their pastor's orthodoxy; and, when he was through, it was understood that any of the ministers of the association were at liberty to relate any conversations or teachings, of which they might have knowledge, that bore on either side of the question.

Being called on to present his charges, Mr. Smiley rose and said, —

"Mr. Moderator, and gentlemen of the council, you will pardon me, if, out of the fulness of my heart, I say one personal word before I proceed to read the paper I hold in my hand. I loved our minister like a brother." Here he stopped, took out and carefully unfolded a scented handkerchief, and delicately wiped his eyes. "Excuse me," he said, "for thus obtruding my personal feelings on a public audience; but you do not know how hard it is to testify against your own minister of the gospel."

"Oh, but he's just an angel, he is!" whispered Mrs. Buck to aunt Sally Rawson.

"Angel a heap!" said Jane Ann, who overheard the aside. "Take my word for it, he's got more hoofs than wings."

"Jane Ann, shet your mouth," said Aunt Sally, "and don't you let me hear you slanderin' yer betters agin."

But Brother Smiley proceeded, —

"Yes, I loved him like a brother. And I wish that it might fall to other lips than mine to speak what stern duty compels me to say." (As a fact, he had log-rolled for the position of prominence and leadership, like a ward-room politician.) "And now," he continued, "I must intimate beforehand that theological looseness is bad enough, — yes, bad enough," he repeated emphatically; "but what shall be said when looseness concerning the gospel issues in its natural results of looseness of life? Yes," he repeated, seeing the sensation his last words created, "looseness of life, my brethren. But, however, let that pass for the present, my brethren. It must come up in its own place. We will attend to one thing at a time; and either one or the other will be enough to sadden all our hearts, — yes, sadden all our hearts, my brethren. Excuse these tears, but nature will have way."

"Oh the old hound!" vehemently exclaimed uncle Zeke to Judge Harrington, as they stood with a little knot of sympathizers just out of the door, in the edge of the vestibule. "I know he's a-lying when he speaks agin Mr. Forrest's character."

"Of course he's a-lying," replied Judge Harrington. "You take that as a matter of course, unless you know the contrary; and in this case the fee is on the Devil's side, and you don't catch him telling the truth unless it pays high."

" Ef the days o' mericles weren't over, we might see Ananias and Sapphiry over agin," added uncle Zeke.

Meantime, sublimely unconscious of comments, and swelling with pious importance, Mr. Smiley continued, —

"First, then, Mr. Moderator, it is my painful duty to present charges and specifications as to his theological soundness; or, to speak more accurately, unsoundness, my brethren. Allow me, then, to read the following paper.

'CHARGE FIRST.

"'The Rev. Mark Forrest, being a minister of the orthodox church, and a member of this association, and pastor of the church in Bluffton, has been unfaithful to his position as a maintainer of the pure faith of the gospel.

"'*Specification First.* — He is in the habit of using very

doubtful language in respect to fundamental doctrines. His trumpet does give a most uncertain sound. For instance, in sundry sermons and prayer-meeting talks, and in essays read at various associations, he has spoken heretically, or neglected to speak at all, concerning the following doctrines, to wit: the fall of man in Adam, and their just condemnation therefore to all the ills that the human race has suffered; the doctrine of total depravity; the atonement through the sacrificial blood of Christ; election by grace; the infallibility of the Bible; and the everlasting punishment of the wicked.

"'*Specification Second.* — He is known to fraternize with such men as Judge Harrington and uncle Zeke on the hill; and when they say they like his doctrine because it is different from the old style, instead of rebuking them, he accepts of their approval.

"'*Specification Third.* — In an essay read at the association held in Slidell, he expressed his belief in the horrible teachings of Darwin and modern science; and, further, in a debate, defended the character of that arch-infidel Theodore Parker.

"'*Specification Fourth.* — At the funeral of the late Mrs. Grey, a notorious infidel, who by guile had won the hearts of many of our young people from the truth, he dared to hold her up as a model; and he accompanied his remarks with certain ill-concealed hits at those who hold to 'salvation by faith,' and do not trust, as she did, to works.

"'*Specification Fifth.* — He has preached against the special providence of God, and assigned matters of his government to natural causes. As, for example, referring to a fire in the neighboring town, he denied that there was any proof that it was a judgment of God; and said that he thought the cow that kicked the lamp over had more to do with it than the sins of the people. And in like manner he has charged diseases on a lack of sanitary care rather than the wrath of God.'

"These, brethren, are enough. We had written out several more; but they are unnecessary. We lay this charge before you for your consideration. I would not prejudice your minds beforehand; and yet it is only fair to intimate that the matter of our second charge is far more serious, so far as his character is concerned, though this one touches far more closely the integrity of the gospel. For one may be a great sinner, — as I fear he is, my brethren, — and yet be forgiven and saved by the atoning blood; but, if the 'foundation be destroyed, what shall the righteous do?'"

And he sat down as though he felt sure that so fitting a Scripture-quotation must touch all right-feeling hearts.

Then followed remarks from various neighboring ministers, telling how they had been scandalized by the position Mr. Forrest had taken at different ministerial and church gatherings. His influence, they thought, over the neighboring part of the State, was unfortunate. And particularly did it appear, that in their several towns, when Mr. Forrest came to speak and preach, various and sundry sinners, never at other times seen in the sanctuary, would come out in full force, and praise his sermons, and say they would go to hear such common-sense preaching as that every Sunday in the year; all of which was to the great detriment of the pure word of life as they dispensed it.

"And," said one, "it is not to be put up with, my brethren. Shall carnal men, led astray by their carnal reason, say the gospel is common sense? It is not common sense, my brethren: it is a mystery, — the mystery of godliness, known only to the elect."

"Yis," said uncle Zeke, familiarly tucking Judge Harrington in the ribs: "that's so. I heard that feller preach onct; and, sure 'nough, *'twas* a mystery, — couldn't make head nor tail out on't."

But now the minister from Maple City, one of those who had urged Mr. Forrest to stand the trial, rose and said, —

"Mr. Moderator, and brethren, it is now time that at least a word were spoken on the other side. There are several of us ministers in this association, who feel that we are on trial as well as Mr. Forrest. If he belongs out of our ministry, then we have no right to remain. We have urged him to stand this trial, that the matter might he brought to a test. We are perpetually being taunted by the men of science, and the freer newspaper press, because, as they say, we orthodox churches allow no intellectual freedom in our pulpits. I have been accustomed to resent and deny this charge. And yet, if Mr. Forrest is to-day condemned, my mouth will be shut, and I shall have to confess, that, so far as this association is concerned, the charge is true.

"What, my friends, has Mr. Forrest done? He has preached a gospel of character and life. Are you ready to confess that you do not want these things preached? Then indeed will the street taunt, that church-morality is below the market, be justified. He has also studied all the modern questions of the world in the light of science and scientific criticism. Can we afford to confess that we are unwilling to have the foundations of our faith examined? The bank that is not willing to have its accounts looked into is the one from which sensible and honest men will withdraw their deposits.

"I, for one, am ashamed of the course which so many churches take with their ministers. Do the pews pretend to have studied and understood all these great themes? The idea is preposterous. And yet, in their ignorance, they undertake to decide as to what the minister shall declare to be true."

"Ugh! the insultin' wretch! To call us ignorant!" exclaimed aunt Sally Rawson, under her breath.

"Give it to 'em! good for you!" chuckled uncle Zeke.

But the minister, unconscious of these "asides," continued, —

"You put a premium on the ignorance and dishonesty of your ministers. You make it a crime to study and learn any thing new; and you make it a virtue in them to cover up and refuse to speak any new word of the Lord that may come to them. You make the bread and butter of their wives and children depend on their echoing your threadbare thoughts, instead of inviting them to go forward and be your leaders. Do you think that God is dead, or that he has no way of getting access to human hearts to-day?

"If the ministers of our churches are not to be per-

mitted to study all through God's universe, and take his truth
wherever they find it as their rightful heritage as his children, then there are many of us who will be glad to find it
out; and we shall discover ways of making for ourselves
platforms where we *can* speak, and where free and brave
and intelligent men and women will listen to us."

A vigorous round of applause followed this brave chal-
lenge. But when the vote was called, stupidity and prejudice — as is usually the case — were found to have a
numerical majority; and Mr. Forrest was condemned as
heretical by a majority of three votes on the part of the
qualified members of the council.

And now Mr. Smiley, with the air of one whose righteous
course Providence had at last justified, arose again. He
pulled out his handkerchief, and prepared for another spon-
taneous display of emotion.

"Brethren," said he, "satisfaction at the vindication of
the cause of the Lord, and sorrow for my erring brother,
contend so for mastery in my soul, that you must not be
surprised if you see me agitated. A righteous judgment
has been reached, my brethren, as to these theological vaga-
ries, in spite of the unwise and ungodly defence of some
whom pride of heart has led astray," he looked around
at the Maple City minister, — "and yet, as I gave you
timely warning, this is not all, my brethren, this is not all.
I might wish that the honor of God's Zion could have been
spared this disgrace; but, my brethren, the ways of the
Lord are mysterious, and perhaps we needed this chastise-
ment. Perhaps, my brethren, only a humble member of

this branch of our common Zion, — perhaps I needed to be humbled by being a member of a church whose minister should do such an unheard-of thing in the camp of the Lord.

"It is now my painful duty, brethren, to read our

'SECOND CHARGE.

"'We charge that the Rev. Mark Forrest, being a minister of the gospel, and pastor of this church in particular, has grossly shamed his office, and brought disgrace upon the cause of Christ, as shall be indicated in the following specifications.

"'*Specification First.* — While on a recent visit to New York, the said Rev. Mark Forrest was seen, by those prepared to testify to the same, to visit a certain house of notorious character, in a disreputable part of the city.'"

"Mark, I'm not going to stand this," fiercely exclaimed Tom Winthrop in a hoarse whisper, where he sat by the side of his friend.

"Yes, you are: keep still," calmly replied Mark.

"But it's an outrage on public decency."

"No matter. I've promised; keep still. *He* can't outrage any decency," said he with quiet contempt. "At any rate, hear him through."

"'*Specification Second.* — This same Rev. Mark Forrest, on leaving New York, travelled in company with an unknown woman, whom he has left concealed at Maple City.

"'*Specification Third.* — And only last Sunday — beside at least one previous visit — he visited this aforesaid unknown woman, and was actually seen in her company.'

"And now, my brethren,"—and he stopped once more to cough, and wipe his eyes, though there appeared a lamentable dearth of moisture,—"my painful duty is accomplished. No one knows so well as my humble self, with what painful reluctance it has been performed. But, my brethren, the Lord's cause must be vindicated, and his Church purged from corruption. I therefore wish to bring this unspeakably painful scene to a close. To that end, with your permission, Mr. Moderator, I will read a resolution which has just been handed me." (He had written it himself that morning, and put it into the hands of a clerk to give to him at the proper time. He wished it to appear as prepared by some one else equally anxious with himself for the purity of Zion.) "This resolution is as follows : —

"*Resolved*, — That it is the sense of this council of ministers and fathers in the Church, that the Rev. Mark Forrest be deposed from the ministry of the gospel, of which he has shown himself unworthy; and that the churches of our common faith be duly apprised of his misdemeanors, and warned that he is not a suitable person to admit to their pulpits."

He had hardly finished reading, when the smothered excitement and indignation broke out ; and cries of "No, no !" "No gag-law !" "Proof, proof !" arose from several parts of the house.

"Why do the heathen rage agin the Lord's anointed ? " piously ejaculated old Mrs. Buck.

"It's a confounded outrage ! " shouted old uncle Zeke.

"Mr. Moderator," called out Judge Harrington, " though not a member of this council, I am a member of this town, and a friend of Mr. Forrest. This is indecent and lawless; and in the name of justice I protest."

The apoplectic face of Mr. Smiley was now flushed and red with disappointment, and then lividly pale with rage. His policy forsook him for a moment; his smile that he *wore* was lost in the underlying deep sea of hate that came to the surface, and swamped it as bubbles are lost in a storm. He tried to gain the ear of the house; but there were enough present who were in no mood to hear him further, to prevent it. In the midst of the general excitement, Mr. Winthrop jumped to his feet, and closed an excited consultation with Mr. Forrest by exclaiming, —

" No, Mark, I'll bear it no longer. This is too much for any promise made in the dark. It's better so. I see daylight now."

He leaped on the platform by the pulpit, and stood silent, pale, and determined. The sight of Mr. Forrest's well-known friend in this unusual position roused everybody's curiosity, and startled the house into sudden silence.

Mr. Smiley looked as though he would like to rend him like a tiger; but policy, — now uppermost again, — and the will of the council, kept him still in his seat.

XIX.

TOM SPEAKS.

"MR. MODERATOR," calmly and deliberately began Mr. Winthrop, "I am perfectly well aware that this is not formal. But this is no time for forms. I am not a member of this council; and without your permission I have no right to speak." — "Go on! go on!" rose in determined cries all over the house. "But I suppose what you want is the truth, something on the basis of which you can render an impartial decision. I happen to be in possession of facts that have a vital bearing on the question before you; but if you do not care to listen to them in this place, from me, I shall find other ways of bringing them to your attention."

At this point Mr. Smiley rose placidly to his feet, and said, —

"Mr. Moderator, this is an unusual and extraordinary proceeding. I protest" —

"Sit down! Sit down!" "Hear Mr. Winthrop! Hear Mr. Winthrop!" "Fair all round, I say!" and other such impatient cries, broke from all parts of the house.

Mr. Smiley saw it was no use, and angrily gave way.

Mr. Winthrop proceeded, —

"If you should not hear me, friends, it would not balk my purpose; and yet I thank you for permitting me to go on."

Mr. Forrest now sat with his face in his hands, and, since he could do no otherwise, let his friend have his way.

He said, —

" I am the life-long personal friend of Mr. Forrest. I am proud of the honor; and I will not see him unjustly harmed, so long as I have power to stand in his defence. Having known him from a boy, I know on what good ground I speak, when I say that he is incapable of a mean or unmanly thing.

"You know me well enough to understand that I do not care to meddle in your purely theological quarrels; though what better a church ever can do than to build up true manhood and womanhood in society, as your minister has tried to help you do, is more than I pretend to understand.

"I think I know enough of the men and passions of Bluffton to know with whom all this trouble has originated."

"Do you mean me, sir?" severely asked Mr. Smiley, who now rose to a point of order.

"Mr. Moderator," continued Mr. Winthrop, "if I am not mistaken, this is an occasion on which personalities that bear on the trial are permitted; and, since the character of a witness has some important relation to his testimony, I am willing to answer the gentleman's question;" and, turning and looking him full in the face, he said, —

"Yes, Mr. Smiley, I mean *you*. And," proceeding rapidly

before he could again be interrupted, "whenever the church will proceed to investigate them, I am ready to present charges that will convince the most prejudiced that it is Mr. Smiley, and not Mr. Forrest, that ought to be on trial."

While this was being said, Mr. Smiley was terribly excited, in spite of his herculean effort to appear the typical meek and lowly disciple. He had on his office-look when only clerks and strangers were in; and all his prayer-meeting face was gone. But his efforts to control himself made him look as though a compressed blood-vessel might burst at any moment.

The scene over the house was one to be remembered. Judge Harrington looked happy; uncle Zeke was radiant; Deacon Putney, the conflict not being settled, did not yet know how he ought to look, and so really did look confused and foolish. Aunt Sally and Mrs. Buck were horror-stricken at an infidel's being in the pulpit, and appeared to expect a lightning-stroke to smite the church for such "goings-on." Jane Ann added to her mother's horror by ejaculations of unregenerate delight at seeing Mr. Smiley getting, for once, what she ambiguously termed "his come-uppance."

But the apparent determination of the house to hear Mr. Winthrop through brought everybody at last to quiet again, and he went on, —

"But the main thing on which I wish to be heard is not a theological one. I happen to know the facts of the visit of Mr. Forrest to New York. He would have kept still, and allowed himself to be condemned through his honorable fidelity to a sacred promise. I also — little knowing that things would come to such a pass as this — had promised to keep his secret. And I might do so even now, did I think the lady's interest would be perilled by my speaking. But, since I now believe otherwise, I cannot allow a true man to be slaughtered by the lying tongue of scandal. I have an interesting story to tell, — a story whose interest may be painful to some before I am through, and that ought to make the ears burn that listen.

"A certain beautiful young lady was the ward of a domineering brother. She lived, no matter where as yet. She was in love with and engaged to a noble man, that this brother opposed. Being of a timid and yielding disposition, and all her inherited property being in her brother's hands, he easily frightened and coerced her to his will. This in all ordinary matters. But even the weakest will sometimes rebel; and when this brother proposed to compel her to marry another man against her will, for the purpose of helping on some business schemes of his own, she fled from home, and went to visit friends in an Eastern city. She would have sent for the one to whom she was engaged, and been secretly married, only that she was too proud to tell him her reasons, and he was not in a business position to make it seem desirable as yet for some time. Meanwhile her brother refused to send her money, and she became despondent. She thought of suicide, or, at any rate, did not seem to care what became of her. Her friends watched her, fearing she might lose her reason. One day she disappeared. They traced her to Fall River, and aboard the New York boat, and then lost the track. She sat up late, and

meditated flinging herself into the Sound. She would walk
the saloon, go out on the deck, and watch the black water
as it sped past, and then, shuddering, enter the saloon again.
This she did several times. She wished for death, but
lacked the resolution.

"She had noticed that she was watched by two men; but
she did not think of fear on a public boat, and she was too
much absorbed in her own sorrow to keep watch of their
movements. Toward midnight, as she passed, with her
head down, by the long rows of staterooms, a door suddenly
opened, she felt herself dragged irresistibly in, and, before
she could open her lips to scream, she was gagged and
bound.

"When she came to herself she awoke in a room most
gorgeously furnished, and, to her horror, discovered what had
passed and where she was. She was an involuntary inhabit-
ant of one of the gilded dens of vice in the great metropolis. Here was something worse than the death she sought.
At first she was frantic: she determined to escape at all
hazards. And then the appalling thought came over her,
that she was branded now, and past hope. No one would
believe her story. They would think she had come there
by her own fault. If her brother had been cruel before,
what would his wounded pride make him now? And she
knew him so well as to feel that perhaps, since she would
not marry the man he had chosen to further his own interests, he would be glad to be rid of her, and so get her fortune
that he now held only in trust. And then her lover, — of
course he was now lost forever: he would never take a wife

whose reputation was tainted. And how could she face the world? They would point their fingers, and hiss through their teeth, in whatever station she might move. What wonder if, under such considerations, her resolution to escape gave way, and she made up her mind to submit to what seemed the inevitable?

"Just now Mr. Forrest was in New York."

At this point the listening was breathless; and Mr. Smiley, in particular, looked on Mr. Winthrop like a fascinated thing. But he went on, —

"He visited at the house of a friend, who is an old physician. He had an patient among this class of women where the poor victim was now a prisoner. One morning as he started on his calls, — if I ever believed in special providences, I should say the Divine Spirit prompted him to invite Mr. Forrest to go with him.

"'Come,' he said, 'I must make a professional call. Go with me, and we can talk as we go.'

"Thus invited, he went. And this is the substance of Mr. Smiley's first specification under his second charge. But more is to come.

"As they passed through the hall, Mr. Forrest caught sight of a face that was familiar from photographs he had seen. Having a singular memory for faces, he was sure he was not mistaken. He looked again; and, astonished though he was, he felt sure of the identity. As the woman passed, he said, looking her full in the face, —

"'Good-morning, Mary.'

Mr. Smiley started as if some one had struck him, but was perfectly still.

"She, not being willing to be recognized in a place like this, looked on him calmly as she could, and said, —

"'My name is not Mary. Why do you speak to me? I do not know you.'

"'Yet your name is Mary,' said he; and she passed on.

"When the medical call was over, and they were returning through the hall again, Mr. Forrest noticed that the parlor door was open; and, as he glanced in, the same woman stood by the mantel, and beckoned to him. Excusing himself from the doctor, he went in, and stood before her.

"'Why did you call me Mary?' said she.

"'Because that is your name,' he quietly replied. 'I have seen your photograph too often not to know you. Why are you here?'

"She knew him also by pictures of him she had seen, though till now she was not ready to acknowledge it.

"'Mr. Forrest,' she said, and broke down, sobbing, 'I am lost.'

"'Perhaps not,' said he. 'Do you want to stay here?'

"'O God, no!' she sobbed; 'but where can I go? what can I do?'

"'Sit down here calmly, and let us talk,' said he.

"When she had told him her whole story, she continued, —

"'But I can't go back to my brother: he'll not take me. The man I was to marry will turn away from me. I may as well stay here. Only don't tell any one where I am,' she desperately pleaded.

"'But, since you do not want to stay here, it is worth while to try what can be done. Go West with me. I will keep your secret till you are ready to speak. I will sound your brother, and find what he will do. I will explain every thing to your lover : he is a man, and will do right.'

"'Perhaps,' she said, 'there is hope. I found myself here only yesterday. I am pure of any voluntary stain. I will let you try ; yes, you may try.'

"And so Mr. Forrest ordered a carriage, took her to a hotel, paid her bills, and has brought her West to my house, where she is now *concealed*, as the second specification charges.

"As to the third, he has been to Maple City to see her. He was in her company last Sunday. He tried to get her consent to speak with her friends ; but, timid and frightened, she would not yet give it. His promise, that, unlike some, he chooses to honor, has kept him silent, and made it possible for his enemies to abuse a man whose shoes they are not fit to carry. Though, did she know now much depended on the words I have spoken, she would have been here herself for the deliverance of her savior."

All eyes were now turned toward Mr. Forrest, who still did not look up ; but, as Mr. Winthrop proceeded, they fastened on him again.

"Only a word more is to be said. That word, I am genuinely sorry and pained to say, must be one of disgrace. But, mind you, the disgrace does not attach to my friend Mr. Forrest. It does, however, attach to him who is the underhand leader and instigator of this whole — not prosecution, but — persecution. It only remains for me to add,

that this young lady, the victim of her brother's avarice and
lack of heart, — a brother who covers his selfish plans deep
down under a sniffling piety, — this mysterious Maple City
lady, now at my house and under my care, is the sister of
your noble prosecutor, Mr. Richard Smiley."

A silence struck dumb with astonishment followed ; and
then it burst into uproarious applause. Uncle Zeke flung
his hat up to the ceiling, and shouted, —

"Hooray ! I knowed he was all right ! I knowed it ! In
course I did ! "

Deacon Putney rushed forward, and grasped Mr. Forrest's
hand ; and he now was thronged by congratulations on every
side.

And even old Mrs. Buck and aunt Sally looked wise,
and mutually remarked in a breath, —

"Of course ! anybody might 'a' knowed such a nice man
as Mr. Forrest was all right ; " and they actually made themselves think they had always been of the same opinion.

But where was Mr. Smiley? He had followed Mr. Winthrop's narrative with breathless and passionate attention.
He had seen the possibility of its conclusion, and shrunk
from it while his heart stood still, as if terror-struck in a tempest. And yet he had hoped it was about some one else ;
and he did not dare to speak, or show his conflicting emo-
tions, for that would be confession at least of a parallel
story on his own part. So he sat in speechless horror as the
tale proceeded ; and when the climax came, he saw, in one
vivid flash of thought, as though his brain had been lighted
by an electric blaze, his power and prestige gone. He was

unmasked. No more in city or church could he be the leader again; and to live, and not lead, was to him worse than death. So, while the confusion raged about him, a worse chaos and struggle went on within. He was flushed and livid by turns; and, as at last he clutched his nails into his palms in the effort at self-control, he suddenly fainted and fell.

A physician who was present was hurriedly called; and he had him taken up, and carried to the door. But when he got there, and felt for his pulse, it was only a flicker; and even that soon ceased. The doctor said a blood-vessel had burst in his excitement. And Richard Smiley was no more.

XX.

THE BROKEN RING.

MR. FORREST cared little for his triumph, — little for the excited change in the feelings of the fickle public, that, by as much as it had degraded him, now exalted him in its enthusiastic reverence as a hero. It was little to him that the church, almost in a body, now came and begged him to stay with them. For, even had he not been condemned as heretic by a formal council, still he felt that in an orthodox church was not his proper field of work. He could not remain without contracting his range of study, and clipping the wings of his thought; and these things he could not do, and maintain his self-respect. For to call it freedom of thought, where you were bound under penalty to come to certain foregone conclusions, now seemed to him a sad intellectual confusion in the use of words, even if you overlooked its reprehensible moral quality.

He cared, I say, for none of these things; for the reason that he saw inevitably before him the darkest sorrow of his life. It seemed to him worse than death: for death leaves tender regret and inspiring memories; and also it leaves one the hope, at least, of meeting again those so rudely torn from us here. But a separation like that which he foresaw was coming was bereft of all these consolations. It could leave behind it only useless, gnawing regrets; and, should they meet in any future, still he would have no claim based on any past possession.

So keenly did he feel this, that he could not nerve himself up to face the meeting and the parting. He must postpone it, and collect himself after his excitement. So, sending Madge a note appointing a meeting for the following Sunday evening, and excusing himself till then, he determined to return with Tom to Maple City.

"I can't bear even to see my friends now," said he. "They will talk to me kindly, but about things of no concern to-day. A husband waiting for the funeral of his wife doesn't care to discuss the market rates."

And so he took himself away. The two days passed quickly, as do the last hours to the criminal awaiting the clock-stroke that knells his execution. Here at Maple City, he walked up and down the levee as the steamer came and went, and thought over the crowded events of this one year. His life seemed short, compared with its hurried events.

"How many tragedies," thought he, "are beginning, progressing, or ending, in the midst of these apparently thoughtless passengers, as they come and go!"

He went over the past, step by step, and lived it all again. He and Tom, two happy, careless young men, stood on the levee once more. They jested together about the little lady that tripped so heart-free up the plank; and now he and that lady dared not look each other in the face, for

the great agony that was tugging at both their hearts. A
little year ago, and he stood on the forward deck, and
sailed out into the fairy world of enchantment, and in that
world he had found the princess of his soul; but the dragon
of old theologic superstition held her in the midst of a magic
circle from which she could escape only over her father's
heart; and this her very goodness forbade. His new-found
friend, Mrs. Grey, was gone. He must clasp the honest old
hand of uncle Zeke, and try to say good-by. His life-work
was blasted. The past had turned to ashes; and the future
as yet was a desolate wilderness, through which he could
not even catch the glimpse of a path.

And now, as he turned away, his soul was wrung with
questionings.

In such a mood as this, — for the past year haunted him,
— he started out in the evening for a lonely walk. He had
talked himself tired with Tom; and for a little, before he
went to bed, he must be alone. He strolled beyond the
edge of the town, and on the bank of the river. The sky
was full of stars, and their far-off silence was as near to sympathy as any thing he could bear. And now the flood swept
over him. Moods changed so rapidly that he seemed to
possess several selves; and now and then he would lose
himself in the fancy that he was listening to a raging contest
in which he had no concern except to hear; and then he
would wake, and come to himself with a new and added pang
of sorrow.

"Oh, I've been a fool!" he cried. "Why need I seek to
be wiser than my fathers? I've tasted the spring of knowl-

edge, and its waters have madness in them. Thousands
have lived and died happy in the old faith. Why need I
undermine the house in which I might have sheltered and
delighted in my love?"

And then he would think again, —

"'The first intellectual and religious houses of the race were
caves and huts. And, as the first steps of upward progress
were made, doubtless the same questions came then from
hearts with the same world-old agony. It is always a crime
to tear down the old, even for the sake of a better. Our
present houses, perchance, are but primeval huts to those
which shall give palatial religious shelter to the men who
shall look upon us as, in comparison, superstitious and bar-
barous. The destructive builders of the past are the ones
we worship, though their ages cast them out. And some
one must do the work of to-day for the future. But need
I do it? Oh that I might escape! But I have heard the
voice of God; and now *woe is me* if I preach not his better
gospel. And, O Madge! woe is me if I do!"

On Saturday the two friends again walked together down
to the boat.

"Mark," said Tom, as arm in arm they strolled slowly
down the street, "I haven't felt like speaking to Miss Smiley
after all that has occurred: how do you find her?"

"As badly as her brother treated her, still, you know, the
ties of blood are strong, and he was the last of her family.
The manner, also, of his taking-off, was a great shock to her.
Still I can't but think she feels a sense of relief. He wasn't
one that anybody could love overmuch."

"And since he has never married, and left no will, she, as next heir, comes now into his property as well as her own."

"Yes; and, best of all, the odious dependence on him, created by her father's will, is of course broken now, and she is free."

"But what does she say, Mark, about my breaking the silence of her secret?"

"Of course her delicacy would have had it kept; but, under the circumstances, she blesses you for it. She up-braided me most severely for not letting her know how my relations to her were complicating my own affairs. I think she'd have appeared at the council, and told her own story, rather than have had me suffer by her silence."

"But now, Mark, it's almost boat-time, and I must ask you a word or two about Miss Hartley."

"O Tom! I can hardly speak on that subject now. She's lost to me forever, I fear. Fear? I know it, Tom. I wish I, too, had fallen beside Smiley. 'Wherefore is light given to him that is in misery, and life unto the bitter in soul?' I've nothing left to live for."

"Why don't she leave the old curmudgeon of a judge, Mark? What's the use of spoiling a living happiness for a dying superstition?"

"Don't speak that way, Tom, if you love me. You don't know the judge, or Madge either. We three are simply the fated personages in an inevitable tragedy. In his circum-stances, the judge could be no other than he is. And of his kind he's a noble specimen, a true man. And, beside, he's too old to change. The brain gets stiff, as the joints do, with age. And, in my circumstances, I can be no other without deliberate surrender of my manhood; and I won't offer Madge a shell with only a lie wrapped up in it. And as for Madge herself, dear, sweet girl, I couldn't change her without spoiling her high womanhood. If she could trample on her father's heart, then by and by she might on mine. No, Tom, it's tragedy. Just as in the old Greek plays the characters are inmeshed by the fates in circumstances where death is the only way out, so it is now. What the gods mean by it all, perhaps we'll know some day; but I can't make it out now."

"Well, Mark, old fellow, I wish I could help you; but it's one of those battles where only one can fight."

Meantime Madge also was struggling alone with her destiny. Mark had been condemned by the council; but she did not know enough of the technical points in dispute fully to appreciate what his awful heresy was. But her heart rose up in admiration of his manliness and sincerity. And particularly did her heart throb with a new and deeper love at the revelation of his tenderness toward the fallen, and his faithfulness to his delicate sense of honor at whatever cost. In her soul she bowed down before the image of his nobility, and worshipped, as one does homage to the figure of some grand heroism in history or romance.

But then, she was one of those whose roots strike deeply into the reverence and sentiment of the past. All she had ever known or thought of God, of duty, of sanctities, of religion in the present, or hope for the future, were linked indissolubly with her father's thought and the training of her home. As she had conceived no other thought, to give up that seemed bald, blank atheism, the blotting all high, sweet spiritualities out of the universe. She knew Mark must see something; but to her it was all chaos and darkness. When she thought of these things as gone, her soul seemed to wander up and down a desert world, like the Wandering Jew, driven on and on; or like the dove from the ark, seeing no place of rest, but only a dreary waste of waters that had buried every sweet and beautiful and green thing. All her childhood memories plead with her. The past rebuked her as an impious traitor. The future threatened; for, having vividly in her mind the whole evangelical scheme of things, her guardian angel seemed to weep for her possible defection. And in her dreams she found herself standing outside the fast-shut gate of the celestial city into which she had just seen father and mother and sisters enter; and, as weeping she turned hopelessly away, she saw Mark, with haggard look and downcast eyes, ready to plead with her for an impossible forgiveness for having led her astray. And, as she waked, she would think that even outside with him was better than any heaven from which his honesty could cast him out. But then her conscience stood up stoutly in her soul; and all her moral, tender, loving nature revolted at the thought of trampling on her father's heart for the sake of gratifying a selfish love.

"No," she cried, "I can not, will not. It may kill me, it will kill me; but I will not be ignoble! If I cannot be a true daughter, I cannot be a true wife. If I am untrue here,

I shall only be giving Mark, not what he seeks, a whole, true woman, but one whose conscience has been violated, the tone of whose life has been lowered."

Such, then, were the two hearts that fate had driven together in the passionate collision of a hopeless love. They could only touch hands, and learn how sweet it was to look in each other's eyes, and then find growing up between them the stern, hard, cold face of Duty, and see her fixed finger pointing them each a separate way.

Their meeting on Sunday evening was a passionate one; for, while Mark held her convulsively to his heart, their tears did eloquent duty for words. They needed only brief speech for mutual understanding. The electric wires of love and grief carry subtle messages, and need not the clumsy medium of language.

"Madge," at last he said, "I must leave Bluffton to-morrow. I cannot endure it here. Let us take one more walk before I go."

And, as they stepped out into the night, they seemed instinctively to feel that there was only one place to which they *could* go, and that, the now sacred spot that had such sweet, and was to have such bitter, memories. They sat down again beneath the old chestnut-tree; while the moon once more came up large and round and yellow in the dense atmosphere that belted the horizon, and looked across the shimmering river full into their saddened faces.

"Madge," said he, as he caressed a loosened lock of hair upon her forehead, "do you love me still, as you did when we sat here before?"

"Don't break my heart with a question like that. I've only learned to love you more and more."

"And yet you cannot follow me," said he with a slight tinge of reproach in his tone.

"Mark, if you loved *me*," she cried almost fiercely, "you would not make it harder for me than it is. It is already more than I can bear."

"But, Madge, I've only done my duty."

"Oh, if you could only have let these awful things alone! It cannot be God that has led you to what is killing me."

"Can you not follow me even yet, since you *do* love me?"

"Oh, I can't, I can't! I dare not! Father has not spoken much of late; but oh, he *looks* at me so! His white face would haunt me forever, could I desert him now."

"But, Madge" —

"Mark!" she broke in hurriedly and abruptly, "do you know what you ask of me? Would you have me at the price of making me unworthy of you? One falsity in life would taint me all through. I can't, I can't!" she sobbed: "do not tempt me, or I shall fall."

"But at the worst, Madge, may I not think of it as a temporary separation? Years of waiting will be nothing, if I may hope."

The struggle now in Madge's soul was fearful. This to her was not a new suggestion. She had battled with it in the long days, and it had haunted her in her dreams. Long before this she thought she had settled it, that she must not

consent even to this. Her father was hale and strong, and
would live for years. Meantime she should change, and
Mark would change. Men loved, she said to herself, then
went away, and learned to love again. So it might be with
him. He would go away, and find another field of activity.
Others would smile upon and flatter him. Meanwhile she
would be losing her freshness as she lived on at home, and
waited on her father's declining years. Her delicate sensi-
tiveness made her feel she would be doing him a wrong to
keep him tied to a promise that anyway must wait for years,
and that he might come to wish himself freed from. She
had said to herself, —

"True love will live without promises; and, though it
break my heart, I must be true to his real interests, even if I
appear cruel. I do not love him as I ought, if I cannot
take up this cross."

So as he repeated his question, —

"May I hope, Madge?" she said slowly, and with a sort
of desperate firmness, —

"Yes, Mark, we will both hope — for the best; for heaven
if not for earth. But here and now we must separate and be
free. It is better so;" and she bit her lips, and crowded
back the tears.

"Madge," he said, rising to his feet, "I had hoped for
more than this."

"Mark," said she, "the years will be many before I am
free. I shall change. You will change. I cannot wrong
you by holding to you a pledge you may wish to break."

"But I can never love any one else," pleaded he.

"The years will tell."

"You will not, then?"

"Mark, not will not: I *can* not; I *ought* not."

"Madge, I cannot think this kind; and it will leave a bitter memory in my heart. I must think you have some motive I do not know." And out of the strong passion of his love, and his bitter hopelessness, he uttered cruel words, that gave him many an after-pang: "I have been told that women were fickle, but I thought it not of you."

She did not reply; for she could not. She dared not trust herself. She would have broken down weeping like a child in his arms. "I have done right," she thought. "The bond must be snapped at any cost."

She now rose, and the two stood a silent moment in the moonlight. At last she held out her hand, — that hand that had brought him to her feet, and was now pushing him away. He caught it, kissed it, and wet it with his tears.

Then she slowly, without trusting herself to look toward him again, began to move away.

"But Miss Hartley," — the distant address stung her, — "I must at least see you to your gate."

"No, please," she faltered. "It is only a little way; and the evening is light. I cannot part with you there."

He flung himself upon the ground, and buried his face in his hands. When he again looked up, he was alone with the pitiless stars.

As that night, after long tossing, at last he lay in a troubled sleep, he dreamed all over the sad tragedy of Jean Ingelow's "Divided," — a poem he had long ago committed to mem-

ory; and ever and ever through his brain there sounded
the sad refrain, —

> " No backward path; ah! no returning:
>   No second crossing that ripple's flow:
>   'Come to me now, for the west is burning;
>   .   Come ere it darkens!'   Ah, no! ah, no!
>
> " Then cries of pain, and arms outreaching —
>   The beck grows wider and swift and deep:
>   Passionate words as of one beseeching—
>   The loud beck drowns them: we walk, and weep."

XXI.

RECONSIDERATION.

THE very next day saw Mr. Forrest's hurried good-by to Bluffton. He could not bear even to see his friends. He could not leave, however, without one last word with uncle Zeke, and one more grip of his honest hand.

"It's mighty rough on me, Mr. Forrest; but it's jest what I expected," said he. "That ar' Sunday mornin' here on the hill, I told ye you's too likely a feller to be a minister; and ye be, fur sich ornery critters."

"Well, uncle, I've done my duty, and paid the price for it. At least I'll take away with me my self-respect."

"'Deed ye will, Mr. Forrest. An' ye'll take away, beside, the lovin' gratitude o' many a poor man an' woman you've helped. An' ye'll take along the daylight o' lots on us that's long sot in darkness for the want o' a little sense in religion."

And, as they parted, uncle Zeke grasped his hand, and almost crushed it in the warmth of his emotion, while he turned his head away, and pretended to be blowing his nose; though, in reality, he was dashing away the moisture from his eyes, that he was ashamed to have his friend see.

He spent one hurried day with Tom; for in his present
mood of mind he did not wish to stay long, even in the
region of Bluffton, — a region now so thronged with unpleasant memories. There being no longer any reason for Miss
Smiley's remaining at Maple City, she was preparing to put
her brother's affairs into the hands of an attorney for settle-
ment, intending herself to return to her friends at the East.
Her parting with Mr. Forrest was such an one as only their
strange relations could have made possible.

"I shall always think of you as my savior," said she.
"It makes me shudder with horror," — and she covered her
face with her hands, as though shutting out some fearful
picture, — "to think of what the future would have been to
me, but for you."

"But I was only human," he replied. "Any one, not a
brute, would save a sparrow from the hawk."

"Nevertheless," she replied, "it was *you* who saved *me*.
I can never forget that. I shall worship you always as my
saint."

Mr. Forrest had some friends in a northern city on the
lake; and he determined to spend a few days there, while
making up his mind what future course to pursue. Drop-
ping into one of the public reading-rooms one morning, he
met two prominent doctors of divinity, belonging to two different but representative branches of the great orthodox
body. He had met them before, on some public occasion,
and so had sufficient acquaintance to form the basis of a
conversation. The daily papers — those innumerable inky
tongues of the goddess Rumor — had caught the echoes of

Bluffton affairs, so that they knew something of what Mr. Forrest had gone through. They were chatting together in one corner of the room as he entered. Rising, and shaking him cordially by the hand, and one of them drawing a third chair into the corner, they all three sat down together.

"So they've been having you on the theological gridiron, have they?" remarked, rather than inquired, the Rev. Dr. Thomes.

"Yes," replied Mr. Forrest; "and they've fried me so well, that I'm completely *done* — with orthodoxy."

"And I think it's a perfect outrage," continued Dr. Thomes, "that there should always be just enough old fogies from the middle ages, in every conference, to kill off any young man that's bright enough to have a new idea. If they can have their own way, they'll condemn the Church to perpetual mediocrity. They seem to think stupidity and piety are synonymous."

"You never said a truer word, Dr. Thomes, in your life," said Dr. Hay. "I don't know of an exceptionally bright man anywhere, who isn't spotted by somebody as a heretic. Nowadays, that only means that he's got, and dares to utter, a new idea."

"And," said Dr. Thomes, "if no new ideas are to be allowed, I'd like to have somebody explain to me how the world is ever to grow any. These theological purists, if they were gardeners, would be cutting off, in the spring, every new leaf and twig, as *innovations;* and seeing to it that the tree staid where it was last year."

"Yes; but," said Mr. Forrest, "after all my painful and

forced attention to the matter, I am inclined to think they are right. Being acquainted with your reputation as what has come, curiously enough, to be called *Liberal* Orthodox, I am not at all surprised at your opinions. But I must differ from you."

"And *I* must differ with *you*," said Dr. Hay. "Now, in your own case, I think you have made a decided mistake. When, as I see by the morning paper, your people gathered about you, and urged you to remain, I think you ought to have done it. You had a good opportunity to help us fight out this battle."

"But," replied Mr. Forrest, "I have come to feel that I have no right to fight the battle in any such Trojan-horse style. Strategy and deception are counted fair in war; but it seems questionable to me, to fight the battles of truth and God in underhand and deceptive ways."

"I do not quite admit your point," said Dr. Thomes. "Has a man no rights in the church in which he was born?"

"Yes," answered Mr. Forrest, — "the right either to remain loyal to it, or to leave it."

"But may he not remain in it and reform it?"

"I think not," said he, "if I understand what you mean by *reform*, — that is, change it to something else. If a man is in a Shakspeare Club, and concludes that he would prefer a Philosophical Society, the simple and honest way would be to leave the first, and organize the second, not undertake to break up the club while still claiming to be loyal to it."

"But doctrines change," said Dr. Hay, "just as modern

Italian has grown out of the Latin. Must one leave his country on that account?"

"No," said Mr. Forrest; "but I wouldn't confuse things that differ. You don't go on claiming that modern Italian is just the genuine old Latin. You call it what it is, and let people take their choice."

"But there are such stupid prejudices on the part of the common people, that they will not hear the whole truth. They have to be led along like children, as they are able."

"But," returned Mr. Forrest, "I think that — if you will pardon me for saying it — the cowardice of the pulpit is responsible for much of the prejudice; at least, for its continuance."

"And yet," said Dr. Thomes, "the minister must preach what people will hear, if he is going to preach at all. If he gets branded as heretical, then he loses all his influence, and his power is gone. If he is prudent, and gives out his new views as they will bear it, then he can gradually lead them into broader ways."

"I have looked all these arguments over; and you are not the first ones that have urged me to act in accordance with them. But I cannot see my way."

"But consider the case of Mr. Blank, now holding his services in our great hall. He's doing an immense good. Occupying as he does a middle position, he draws about him the conservative liberals and the liberal orthodox, and holds the throngs of both in his hands."

"I know it all, and have thought of it all," Mr. Forrest replied. "And if one, in all honesty and sincerity, can hold such a position, he will appeal to the largest numbers in these transition times. For, let a man be pronounced and clear on either side, and of course he loses those on the other. The times are hazy; and the hazy man, Mr. Facing-both-ways, will see the biggest houses, for he has the largest constituency. An honest Facing-both-ways may do much temporary good. But they are not the builders: they raise only temporary huts till the house gets framed and boarded in."

"If they can hold the position honestly, you said," broke in Dr. Hay: "don't you think they are honest?"

"Some of them, undoubtedly. But it's a strain on any man's conscience. Now, this Mr. Blank you spoke of said only the other day to a friend of mine who was visiting the city, 'Mr. Winthrop, what I think and believe in my study is one thing; and what I think it best, as I consider the condition of my people, to give them as food, and to build them up in the Christian life, that is another thing.' What do you call that?"

"I'm too much astonished to call it any thing," said Dr. Hay.

"But I call it the worst kind of Jesuitry," said Mr. Forrest; "lying for the glory of God, and to build up his kingdom of truth. And yet pardon me for saying that it seems to me only the logical carrying-out of your own principle. Were you not just urging me to do the same?"

"I was not looking at it in that light," said Dr. Thomes.

"Now, let me give you my opinion just a little at length," said Mr. Forrest. "Catholicism, for example, is a fixed and definite system. To change it is, of course, to make something else out of it, to destroy it. The something else may be better; but it certainly isn't the same. To change it all over, then, and still call it Roman Catholic, would be an absurdity as well as a falsehood. Therefore it seems to me that Pius IX. was clear-headed and logical when, in his last encyclical, he anathematized those who said the Church ought to progress, and conform to modern civilization.

"And the same is true of orthodoxy in any form. It claims to be based on a clear, explicit, and finished scheme of divine revelation. Now, the world may change in its relations toward an infallible revelation; but to say that *it* can change, either to retrograde or advance, is simply confusion of thought, or misuse of language. If, then, orthodoxy ever was orthodoxy, — the true doctrine, — then it must remain so forever. There can't be any progress in the facts of the multiplication-table. But if you admit that orthodoxy has changed, or can change in any degree, then it isn't orthodoxy any longer: it admits no past mistake. If there was a past mistake, then there is no certainty but there may be one now. You're all afloat. Instead of orthodoxy, it is rationalism, or the application of reason to all the problems involved."

"But may not orthodoxy grow like a tree?" asked Dr. Hay.

"No, I think not," replied Mr. Forrest. "If last year an infallible revelation had fixed the number of boughs and leaves for a maple, it would have no right to vary. And I cannot help feeling that this whole movement called Liberal

Orthodoxy is a misnomer, a mongrel, that has no right to exist. If it is liberal, it cannot be orthodox; and, if it is. orthodox, it has no right to be liberal. It is very like that often-mentioned but rather mythical creature, the *white blackbird*. It seems to me to be a logical vagrant, without the slightest 'visible means of support.' If one believes in the Garden of Eden and the fall of man, then, of course, the incarnation, the atonement, heaven and hell, logically follow. It is a linked chain; it is a complete logical arch. But Liberal Orthodoxy knocks the keystone out, and thinks the rest will stand. It snaps out one link, and thinks the chain will still hold the clear-headed thinkers of the world. It knocks the foundations out from under its house, and then proceeds calmly up stairs and sits down as if nothing had happened. Such feats are only possible in castles in the air. But men will knock their brains out against logical impossibilities, and still go on unconscious of any accident.

"I know I am preaching you a long sermon; but just think of it. Here are men in every direction, who think they are orthodox, who do not believe in any fall. They. know too much of modern science to still believe the traditions about an apple's bringing death and total depravity into the world. And yet, if there wasn't any fall, there isn't the slightest need of any incarnation or atonement; and the whole scheme of orthodoxy tumbles like a card house."

"But," inquired Dr. Hay, "must the whole orthodox body be deprived of the light of all later knowledge, just because it is orthodox?"

"If it will *stay* orthodox, yes; but if it chooses to accept

modern knowledge, and give up this and that doctrine, then
let it be honest enough to own that it is not orthodox.
Now, there's a great excitement just now over the question
of hell. The moral sense of civilization, having got too
clear-sighted and true to be able any longer to think God is
a devil, of course has to give up hell. But why can't men
see that they can't give up hell, and still keep all the rest?
If man is under natural moral laws of invariable justice and
inevitable execution in this and all worlds, so that he goes
up or down as he gets sick or well, according to character
and conduct, then, of course, a sacrificial atonement by a
dying God is absurd. Redemption, atonement, and all such
ideas, are outgrown.

" And of course it also becomes absurd to hold to the
divine inspiration of a book that plainly teaches doctrines
that are given up. However perpetual some of its moral
precepts, it is henceforth only a human book, a record of a
past phase of the world's religious life."

" But," remarked Dr. Thomes, " I think we'd better hold
to the Bible till the world gets a better book."

" Certainly," replied Mr. Forrest, " by all means. But
let's tell the truth about it at the same time. Give it to men
for what it is, not what it is not. It's curious how men hold
the Bible."

" Why, what do you mean? " said the doctor again.

" I mean this : its infallibility really means to them the
infallibility of the interpretation put upon it by their sect.
So you've really got as many Bibles as you have sects. And
then they hold tenaciously to hosts of things the Bible does

not enjoin, or even forbids, as the keeping of Sunday; and at the same time universally practise what it everywhere condemns, as usury for example. Where would be the support of the churches if the members never took interest on their money?"

"But," said Dr. Hay, "not every thing in the Bible is intended to be perpetual. Some of it is local and temporary."

"There you have it again," said Mr. Forrest. "That's rationalism pure and simple. If reason picks and chooses, then reason decides."

"Well, we differ on these points," said Doctor Hay; "but now tell us where you propose to go. If you can't stay in Liberal Orthodoxy, will you go to the Unitarians?"

"I hardly know as yet."

"He'd find them, in many cases, more bigoted than we are," said Dr. Thomes. "I know many a Liberal Orthodox who would lift the hair of some of the old-line Unitarians like 'quills upon the fretful porcupine.' There's so much bigotry in the world, that you can't keep it all in any one denomination."

"But that isn't my chief objection," said Mr. Forrest.

"What, then?"

"Why, this: Textual Unitarianism or Universalism, that builds itself on verses of Scripture, and claims to be a fixed system, however broad, I can have nothing to do with."

"How broad must a church be, to suit you?" inquired Dr. Hay.

"Just the width of the universe of God. I don't expect

to occupy it all at once. But, so far as I am able, I claim the right — for all of any man — to go wherever God has been before me."

"What's your Bible, then?"

"All ascertained truth, however and wherever found."

"You say all *ascertained* truth. Don't you believe in faith?"

"Yes, as faith; but not as knowledge. I believe in not abusing the dictionary. I *believe* a lot of things I do not know: so I call those things *beliefs*. I am not aware that I *know* any thing that I don't *know*. I don't know much; but I keep the word *knowledge* for that little."

"You have a short creed, then."

"The universe is large. The brain is small. I am willing to stand on what little I know, and work out from that. I value less than I used to my theological possessions 'in Spain.' Eternity is long: I can wait.'

When he had gone out, the Rev. Dr. Thomes and the Rev. Dr. Hay looked at each other, and one nodded while the other said, —

"A clear-headed fellow. Yes; but he carries things a little too far. It won't do. You can't get the people up to it. He goes too far."

XXII.

THE REVENGE OF SLIGHTED LOVE.

THREE years had now passed away. Miss Hartley had devoted herself untiringly to her father's comfort and happiness. She had anticipated all his wants, and done her best to make his home sunny and bright. He had for her a tender, almost a doting love. And thus, though he had rejoiced at her separation from Mr. Forrest, as an escape from a threatened peril to her soul, he still could not avoid a constantly questioning anxiety as to whether she yet carried any lasting wound. So, as these three years passed, he watched her. He was too proud to show curiosity, and too respectful toward her right of silent reserve to ask questions. But though there never fell from her lips, in his hearing, one word of regret or complaint, he could not help noticing that the old spontaneity of her gladness was gone. It was no change of feature, but only a paling of the light that shone behind the features. Her bird-song was hushed, or tuned to a minor key. She did and said the same things as ever; but, instead of bubbling like a spring, her life seemed moved by the machine-pressure of duty. He noticed that in the mornings, as the months went by, something of the old freshness was out of her face. A dark-colored line grew beneath her eyes, like a pen-stroke under a word, to emphasize her sadness. Sometimes, when he came upon her suddenly, he would find her standing with a far-away, absent look on her face; or she would quickly dash away a tear, and start up with a forced smile. Her friends noticed that she cared less for their society, and was less forward in the season's entertainments. And now and then Jane Ann Rawson would remark to her mother, —

"I think it's a burnin' shame! Madge Hartley's jest a-dyin' by inches for Mr. Forrest. Anybody 't 's got half an eye can see it. 'F that old sour-face of a judge 'd only minded his own business!"

"Yis," said aunt Sally, who, now that he was gone, only remembered Mr. Forrest's good qualities, while the present angularities of the judge were easily seen: "sich a nice man as he was! He was too good for any of the tribe o' sich a sharp-cornered old hard-head as he is."

So all the old ladies who used to say "Margaret Hartley was reskin' her immortal soul for a carnal affection," now bestowed all their useless sympathy on the separated lovers when it was too late. They were good-natured old souls, only lacking any rational stability. They were blown about by the veering gusts of their passionate whims, as paper kites are whiffled around by every current of air.

Margaret kept up bravely so long as she was with others, or any demand was made upon her. But in the night her struggles came, and she fought with the memories of the past. After she had locked herself in her chamber, she would sit by the hour like a statue at her window, where she could see what was once *his* window, from which used, in those glad young mornings, to come across the way his manly greeting. Then, from her side-window, she could see in the shadow, the top of the old chestnut, reaching above the crown of the hill, where they met and parted. She would look, and look; and then clasp her hands over her eyes, as if to shut out what she could bear no longer to see. Sitting thus, she burst out at last, as she had done many times before, —

"Oh, I was cruel that night! and yet I couldn't help it. It was not I. Fate spoke through my lips words that I hated. And he — he must have known it! He can't be so blind! He must have known how I loved him. I can't endure the thought that he went away with the feeling that *I* was cruel. And yet it *had* to be so. Something *is* cruel, to play such games with human hearts!"

Then she would sit, and go over all that long year. She felt again the sensation of guilty, glad surprise at having heard those words spoken to her supposed unconsciousness after her fall. Again she looked up with pride, as he spoke his brave, manly words from the pulpit; and she remembered how she felt they were *her* words, for he was hers. She lived over once more the afternoon in which he had read his verses; and she recalled how, while she shrunk from having him avow himself just then, still she had exulted in seeing his heart at her feet. Her whole life now seemed divided only into two parts. She had not *lived* at all till she met him. Then there had been one bright year; and all since then was a wilderness.

She knelt down to pray, as she had always done since her unconscious childhood at her mother's knee.

"O God!" she cried, "must it have been? Is there no pity in heaven for broken love on earth? Canst thou not help me even now? But" — springing to her feet, as the thought flashed over her — "it was religion that took him from me! How can I hope for help from the God that tore us apart?"

And then her heart would stand up, and cry out that it could be no true religion that would so harden and cripple the life. Thus, from such experiences, were born many sceptic questionings as to the principles of her father's faith. She came to ask herself often as to whether Mark was not right.

Then she would get books, and read and think and study. Thus, as the years went by, her outlook grew broader. And, though she had no hope of ever seeing Mr. Forrest again, she was gradually getting nearer and nearer to a possibility of understanding and sympathizing with his thought.

And now at last her father fell sick. It was a long and wasting fever. Night and day she directed all things, and watched him. He was too old, and his vigor too much exhausted, to resist the attack. When the fresh sod was above him where he slept on the hillside above the everlasting flow of the river, Margaret herself was sick. The physician told her she had no organic disease that his medicine could reach: she was only worn; needed to throw off her bur-

dens, and rest. There was nothing to keep her. Her sister
Sue had been a year married to Mr. Snyder, and the
younger sister could stay with her. More, then, because
there was no reason for doing any thing else in particular,
than that she either cared for or expected any thing from
the change, it was decided that she should visit California,
and spend some months at the house of an old aforetime
Eastern friend of her father's.

For two reasons I shall not describe the journey. It is
already familiar in many books of travel; and, further, we
are concerned at present about her inner life. And, should
I describe only what she saw, it would be hardly worth
while; for she was in no mood for sight-seeing, and cared
but little for the natural wonders through which she passed.
While, then, the engine puffed on day after day, whirling her
across plains, around the craggy edges of the mountains,
through tunnels, and past great new cities, toward a new
future, she sat wrapped in her thought, and living in the
past.

She got out at a station in a beautiful valley: there was
no city, and what could be called even a village only by
courtesy. She glanced about her, and saw in the near distance a section of a bay; around her spread a level valley
a mile in breadth from bay to foot-hill, springing from which
was a chain of irregular mountains stretching parallel with
the bay, and forming the other side of the valley. The valley itself was covered irregularly here and there with scattered clumps and groups of live-oaks, ranging from clusters
of three to several hundreds. Instead of city or village

there, it was a place of villas or country-seats such as she
had never seen at the East.   Here lived the wealthy gold or
silver kings of the great Occidental metropolis.   Climbing
up on the foot-hills, or rising above the oak tree-tops, she
caught glimpses of fanciful towers ; and everywhere were
the strange new vans of the windmills that she had never
seen before.

Her father's old schoolmate met her at the station, and
gave her so cordial a welcome that she felt at once as though
she should be more at home here than in places that were
thronged with the ghosts of painful associations.   If she
could only forget the past, here were all the external mate-
rials for a paradise.   But she was learning now, what so
many in all ages had learned before her, that heaven and
hell are in the heart, or nowhere.

It was a charming spot in the foot-hills to which she was
driven.   Perfect in natural beauty, the place had all the
added charm that the landscape-gardener's art could give it.
Winding walks and drives ;   arbors ; rustic bridges and
mimic waterfalls ;   trees of every latitude, in their native
forms, or cut into all weird, fantastic, and beautiful shapes ;
the wide, fresh stables, carriages, harnesses, horses ; foreign
and domestic animals, wild and tame ; birds for sweet song,
or beautiful plumes ; a spacious house with endless piazzas,
with rustic chairs and hammocks ; odd gables, and fanciful
turrets, and hanging windows, and angles that gave out-
looks toward every fair thing that came in range of the eye,
— such was now her home.

But the irrevocable past haunted her.   It made a part of

every landscape. It shimmered with the ripples on the surface of the bay. It sat by her side in her drives. It lurked in every clump of trees. It was a part of the lonely mountain summit. It was her waking dream; it was her night vision.

One day they made a little party to visit the summit of the mountain. Back through the foot-hills to the very feet of the mountains themselves, there ran, or rather wound and twisted, a creek. It was low and clear in summer, but in the rainy season full and turbid. It was now in June; and it ran part-way full, and cool and clear. For four miles the road followed the windings of the creek. The road itself was arched with trees so completely, that for the whole way there was no sight of the blue sky, except through the irregular breaks in the green. Sun-flecked, and carpeted with leaf-shadows, the road was a fairy turnpike into a fairy world. Here and there, as they turned some new curve, the gray limestone cliff, wrought by the elements into some fantastic shape or almost human form, would spring into view through the green trees, fifty feet up the side of the gorge that on either hand hemmed in the narrow valley.

At the end of the four miles was a green glade, a lovely, open spot, where were a hotel and a group of cottages, that had grown up about a mineral-spring. From this point they struck the direct ascent. This was by a fine turnpike that wound about the mountain, doubling on itself, and going two or three miles of turnings to bring the party to a point just above where they were half an hour before, and so near the road along which they had passed that they could fling a pebble over into it.

When they reached the summit, the scene that burst upon them was magnificent beyond the painting power of words. Twenty miles northward the mountain-range ran, and terminated in the promontory on the bay-ward slope of which lay the metropolis of the Pacific, revealing its location by the cloud of smoke that hung above it. To the left, and sweeping every way to the far horizon, lay and shimmered and glistened the wide ocean, its surface heaving in the long and restless roll of the sea, but unbroken by a single ripple. A sail here and there suggested the far-off ports all round the world. Turning to the right, there was first the San Francisco Bay, an unbroken reach of water forty-five miles long, and from four to fifteen in breadth. On both sides of the bay, the valley stretched, dotted with native oak-woods and ranches, and homes and vineyards, and orchards of every fruit from pole to tropic, cut with creeks, and threaded with roads. At intervals, towns and cities sprang in sight on both sides the bay, and spires lifted white above the green of trees. In the distance was San José; and, sweeping round beyond the bay, another range of mountains, with old Monte del Diablo king above them all.

"Do you see that grove of oaks over yonder, and looking as if it were almost at our feet?" inquired Mr. Harrold, her host.

"Yes."

"Well, ten miles away on an air-line, that is now your home."

" Can it be possible ? "

" Not only possible, but a fact."

" But this, it seems to me, must be as fine a view as earth can show.   I never dreamed of any thing so grand."

" Of course we Californians think it cannot be sur-passed."

" And I am a Californian now, so far as that opinion is concerned.   But what is that smoke just outside the Golden Gate there ? "

" An incoming steamer from somewhere.   Probably from Oregon or China ; for, if it were on the Panama line, it would have passed by here."

And then a pang of remembrance shot through her heart as she thought of Mark, who, when last she heard of him, had sailed for some far-off port.   And as she thought of meetings and partings, of the tragedies of human life, woven into its web by the flitting shuttles of swift-passing steamers and cars shooting to and fro over the earth, there ran through her brain the old, sad lines, —

" A ship comes up from under the world.
   ' What do you bring, O ship ? ' he cried.
   The answer came : ' 'Neath flag unfurled,
      Laughter and song, and — a fair dead bride.

" ' I bring fool's jests, and — a heart's deep woe ;
      News of a friend, and — a word of despair ;
   I bring bright hopes from the world below,
      And a soul storm-tossed and worn with care.

" ' I bring a child whose mother is dead ;
      I bring a man deserting his wife, —
   Light and shadow, and poison and bread,
      The tragical comedy of life.

" ' Perhaps I bring a gift for you;
  .   But do not covet it, do not shrink:
  You know not whether 'tis false or true,
    Or better or worse than you can think.' "

She roused from the mood with a deep-drawn sigh.

" What is it? " said Mr. Harrold. " In a day-dream? "

" I was thinking," she replied, " what freightage of good
and evil, of hope and fear, those steamers carry. Who
knows what of dread or joy that ship may be bringing to
land? "

" Has it any thing for you, do you think? "

" No. My ship has gone down, I fear. If not, I do not
know on what sea it sails."

She answered gayly, but meant more than she cared her
tone should betray. Could she have seen the deck as the
steamer drew up to the dock, would she have been glad, or
sorry? Who knows?

The next Monday morning, when the mail came down
from the city, she took up the "Alta" to glance over the
news. Then she hurriedly dropped it, turned pale, and
hastened to her room. Mrs. Harrold picked up the paper,
and looked it over to see what affected her so, but could
find nothing. But she read listlessly the following item : —

    • The Rev. Mark Forrest, just arrived per steamer from China,
preached yesterday in the Free Presbyterian church, on the Ethnic
Religions as related to Christianity."

Laying down the paper, she merely remarked, —

" I do not see any thing here that concerns Margaret."

XXIII.

ADRIFT.

IT was in the year 1864 when Mr. Forrest left Bluffton. "If I cannot be engaged in the *cure* of souls, at least I can in the *care* of bodies," said he to himself; and thus saying, he threw all his energy into the work of the Sanitary Commission in the South-West. Through his experiences here we shall not care to follow him. We only need to know, that, in his present mood of mind, he did not care to spare himself; and that, if any was to do dangerous work, or occupy a dangerous post, he rather sought than shunned the opportunity. He was too manly to seek death; and yet he was compelled to confess to himself that he did not care to flee from it. If it came in the way of duty, he would welcome it as a friend. He had been trained as a minister, and all his tastes ran that way. And yet an impassable wall seemed to shut him out from any farther progress in that direction. And, even if a way had been open, it seemed to him he could not walk it without the face of Margaret Hartley by his side. Sometimes he would have moments of anger at her apparent coldness during their last interview; and yet he held her in too high respect to believe she was capable of caprice.

"Whether I understand her or not, or agree with her or not," he would think, "I *know* she is incapable of giving any one causeless pain. She did only what she thought was duty."

So he could not invent even a poor excuse for either anger or hate. She still nestled in his heart, the one fair image of the only woman he had ever loved. But this image was only a memory, sinking farther and farther down the horizon of the past, — a setting and not a rising star : so he had not even the inspiration of hope. At least, however, he could help the wounded, and write out the last love-messages of the dying. To this best comfort for a hopeless sorrow, — the consolation of helping bear the burden of another, — he now devoted himself.

He followed the march of Sherman to the sea. Thence he came North to assist in the last battles and marches, and see the sword of Lee given into the persistent hand of Grant. But when the last shout of triumph went up, and the war was over, he again found himself with nothing to do, and his heart only sorer with its still unhealed hurt. Going on to New York, he sat down and wrote Tom : —

NEW YORK, —— 186-.

DEAR TOM, — The war is over, and I can be of no more service here. Nothing opens to me as yet ; and, even if it did, I am now fit for nothing. I shall recover my balance some day, and be man enough to pick up some life-work, and pay the world for my standing-room and the lunch I get from the common cupboard. But meanwhile I am off, — nobody knows where, and nobody cares ; least of all, myself. In a couple of weeks I shall sail for Europe ; and then go nowhere in particular and everywhere in general. I am going to attempt the impossible, — to get away from my shadow. The effort will amuse me, if nothing else; and I may stumble on to experiences and information that will be of service to me — when I come to myself. I shall be hard to keep track of after I am aflight; and you may not often hit me with your letters. But let me hear from you once more before I sail. I need not tell you what I most care to know.

Not quite myself, but always the same to my old friend,

MARK.

The answer soon came.

MAPLE CITY, —— 186-,

MY DEAR OLD FELLOW, — You're not the man I take you for, Mark, if you allow any woman that lives to crush the heart out of you. Remember, "there's good fish in the sea as ever was caught." And yet I suppose it's hard for me to sympathize with you. My wife — God bless her! — was stupid and prosaic enough to fall right into my arms in the most natural way in the world: so that I haven't any romantic and heart-breaking experience by which I can interpret yours. They say, "The course of true love never did run smooth;" but mine runs so smoothly, that, if the proverb is true, there must be some defect in the quality of my affection.

But you know, Mark, you have my deepest love and sympathy. I'd gladly give up a part of my comfort if I could transfer the title to you. Be brave, old fellow, and "fight it out on this line," however long it takes.

I'm glad you're going away; though, now I've known you again, I shall be confoundedly lonesome. But it will do you good. So may the winds blow you to some harbor where you will find as good as you've lost!

The last I heard of Miss Hartley, she was living quietly with, and taking care of, the old judge. They say she's just a trifle sadder, and looks worn; but otherwise I hear of nothing.

You will be glad to learn the end of your adventure with Miss Smiley. Hank Tyler, the man I told you she was engaged to before you

found her, like the true fellow I thought he was, has married her, and
they are living in Colorado. She has come into her own and her
brother's money; and "the days of her mourning are ended." She
has your photograph in her chamber; and, I think, worships you as
her saint.

Now Mark, my dear boy, good-by. If in your wanderings you do
not

> "Suffer a sea-change
> Into something rich and strange," —

Keep me posted, as well as you can, of your doings. And, when you
"drop anchor," hoist a signal for

Your old friend,   TOM.

Beyond the mere curiosity of travel, the thing that most
interested Mr. Forrest was, naturally, a study of the practical
phases of the religious life of the countries he visited. Every
man — lawyer, farmer, artist, doctor, merchant — carries
about him his own personality and training, and necessarily sees the world through his own eyes. If he doesn't
always "talk shop," still it is inevitable that he will *see* shop
and *feel* shop. So, as Mr. Forrest was a minister, he looked
over the world with a minister's eyes. The evil of this is
when the manhood withers into a mere profession, instead
of wielding the profession as the sculptor handles his chisel.

He had run through France and Spain, and stood at last
in Rome. Here he met an American gentleman. Talking
over their views of things one day, Mr. Forrest remarked, —

"There's one thing, Mr. Gordon, that strikes a religious
man strangely; and that is, to observe that these European
countries that have the most Christianity are the least moral
and intelligent."

"Why, what do you mean?" he asked with some astonishment.

"I mean what I say. The independent intelligence that makes the freedom and civilization of England and America seems to loosen the grip of the Church, and to tend toward individuality and scepticism."

"But that which you thus criticise is not Christianity. Look at Rome. Do you call this flummery Christianity? It is the Roman-Catholic corruption of Christianity," said Mr. Gordon.

"At least, I think the question has two sides," replied Mr. Forrest. "You can regard any system of religion as a doctrine, or an institution."

"How?"

"Why, when we speak of Buddhism, for example, we may mean the simple moral teachings of Sakya, or we may mean practical Buddhism as it really exists. We judge Buddhism by the effects of the system as it actually works to-day. Why not treat Christianity in the same fashion?"

"Well, explain a little more, and perhaps I'll see what you're after."

"So be it. We Protestants — a little minority of Christendom — go back and say that Christianity is only the precepts Jesus taught. Unitarians go farther yet, and pick out the Sermon on the Mount, or the Golden Rule, and say 'That's all there is of Christianity,' and then denounce the Catholic growth of all the Christian centuries as a parasite."

"And isn't it so?"

"Is a parasite usually larger than the whole tree? Is a

tree simply the roots, or the total development of those roots and the surrounding circumstances? When the Church was organized, it was 'called Christian at Antioch;' and why isn't the natural result of the growth of seventeen centuries to be called Christianity?"

"You think that Roman-Catholicism, then, is true Christianity?"

"I do not see why not, as truly as the present institutions and practices of Buddhism are to be regarded as true Buddhism. When we speak of so-called heathen nations, we think we treat them fairly by pointing to the life of the common people who profess them as illustrating their natural effects and value. If we treat Christianity that way, then it will fare as hardly as most religions of heathendom; while, if we treat the heathen religions as we want Christianity treated, — that is, judge them by the best utterances of their highest and purest minds, — we shall find them more nearly on a level with our own faith."

"You think Christianity, then, no better than Buddhism," said Mr. Gordon.

"By no means. But I think they should be treated equally; judged, in both cases, either by their best or their worst. And I further think, that, when we speak of what Christianity has done for civilization, we ought to remember what civilization has done for Christianity. If Christianity does it all, why isn't the Christianity of the Turkish Empire up to the level of Boston? And how does it happen that the constituted expounders and defenders of Christianity have persistently fought, so long as they could, almost all the growing elements and forces that make up modern civilization?"

"But have they?"

"Please point out an exception. The ruling orthodoxy never yet originated a new thing for civilization, and never accepted it till it had to."

"Holding such views as this, how do you account for the fact that religion is always the foundation and bulwark of morality, on which all civilization rests?"

"I don't account for it : I deny it. It is so far from the truth, that the leading moral sense of the world is frequently in advance of any form of instituted religion. And naturally so ; for institutions stand still, or try to, while the moral sense of the world is a growth that each new year puts forth new leaves. Otherwise there would be no hope of any better future."

This conversation is quoted merely as a specimen of one of his states of mind, and of the critical spirit with which he looked upon society and religion in the lands through which he travelled.

Having visited Egypt, and passed through Palestine, he determined to make a tour of the world. So by the Suez Canal he made his way to Calcutta. Thence he passed to Hong Kong. Making what study he could, or cared to, of the life and religions of India and China, he took steamer for San Francisco, and, as we have already seen, entered the Golden Gate little thinking what eyes were watching the ship from the mountain summit far down the coast.

When in California years before, he had known a Presbyterian minister, at that time strong in his orthodoxy. He was surprised and pleased to learn that he had now abandoned his old position, and had established a flourishing liberal society, under the title of "The First Free Presbyterian Church of San Francisco."

Thinking he would like to go over old times with him, trace the growth of his thought, and find how nearly they were at one, he called upon him. He found him, not fairly sick, but confined to the house, and somewhat troubled as to the supply of his pulpit for the next Sunday.

"If it was an orthodox church," said Mr. Brimmer, "I could find a man to preach for me on any street-corner. But men that will stand in a free pulpit are rare. Now, you must preach for me."

"But how can I?" said Mr. Forrest. "I haven't preached these three years; and, besides, I haven't a sermon."

"Must you have a written one?"

"No. I can talk, after a fashion, if I have any thing to say. But the only thing I've been thinking of in a religious way, of late, is, the characteristic points of the heathen religions, and their relations to Christianity."

"But that's capital. Why won't you talk on that? Nothing would suit my people better."

"Well, if it will help you out, I'll try it."

And so the next Sunday he stood once more in the pulpit. But how were all things changed! His old friends thought he had given up all. He felt that he had gained all. God was no more an exclusive God, and religion no

longer a petty squabble of sects. The universe was his
Bible; of which the old Hebrew and Christian Scriptures,
still dear and sacred, were, after all, only chapters.

He announced as his subject, "The Natural Development of Religions." As a part of his lesson, he read "The
Problem" of Emerson; and he gave special emphasis to the
words, —

> "Not from a vain or shallow thought
> His awful Jove young Phidias brought;
> Never from lips of cunning fell
> The thrilling Delphic oracle :
> Out of the heart of Nature rolled
> The burdens of the Bible old;
> The litanies of nations came,
> Like the volcano's tongue of flame,
> Up from the burning core below.—
> The temples *grew* as grows the grass.
> The word unto the prophet spoken
> Was writ on tables yet unbroken.
> One accent of the Holy Ghost
> The heedless world hath never lost."

Then he developed the idea, that all religions are the natural growth of the religious nature of man : that no one
is supreme above all others by virtue of any supernatural
pre-eminence ; but, if it be supreme at all, it is so only as
one man or one nation surpasses another, or as one tree
overtops all others in a forest.

And, as he looked over the report in the "Alta" the next
morning, what would he not have given to know what other
eyes had been startled by his simple thought, and then in
secret been blinded by tears !

XXIV.

A STRANGE MEETING.

MR. HARROLD and the Rev. Mr. Brimmer were intimate friends. They were frequently together, both in town and at the country-seat of the former.

So on Monday, when Mr. Forrest called on his friend to see how he was getting on, and after they had talked a while on general topics, Mr. Brimmer said, —

"Are you tied up with any engagements this week?"

"No," he replied: "unfortunately I am not tied up to any thing these days. I am the Wandering Jew; and my only limitation is, that I shall not keep still anywhere for long."

"When you were on the coast before, did you know any thing of the San José Valley?"

"I have only passed through it hurriedly; but I saw enough to learn that it's a paradise."

"Well, then, I've a pleasant day for you, if you like."

"Why, what is up?"

"You see, Harrold, one of our leading bankers, has the perfection of a lovely villa down the bay. He's an old friend of mine; and on Thursday — I'll be out by that time — a party of friends is going down to his place for the afternoon. I am at liberty to take any one along I please. Wouldn't you like to go?"

"What's to be done? and who's to be there?"

"Oh! it will be only a quiet knot of right pleasant people, ladies and gentlemen. And there will be bowling and billiards and croquet and walks and drives, — if any one pleases, — and lounging under the trees. The only law is, that you must do just as you've a mind to, make yourself at home, and be happy."

"Well, that's a pleasant programme. I think I'll join you."

So it was arranged. Thus the great world swings round, wantonly flinging us apart, and as wantonly tossing us near again; as the wind scatters and then piles up the autumn leaves.

Meanwhile Mr. Forrest received his mail from the East, and in it a short note from his old friend Mr. Winthrop. And while he reads we will look over his shoulder, and copy one brief extract.

"If it has not already come to hand, you will very soon receive a letter from New York, that will be worthy of your most serious attention. A party of wealthy and intelligent gentlemen in that city, having become dissatisfied with the existing churches, have determined to form a religious society that shall be fearless enough to face the light, and competent to deal with the living movements of the age.

"They have every thing for immediate organization, except a minister. They have heard of you, and the battle you fought out here. It so happened that the leading one of their number is a business acquaintance of mine; and, finding that you and I were old chums, he has

written me about you. Knowing my love for you, and my admiration
for your course, you will readily understand what sort of character
I have given you. I have also hinted to him, that your fitness for such
a task will be very largely enhanced by your journey, observation, and
study.

"As soon as I received your last letter, and learned the probable
date of your arrival in San Francisco, I sent him notice at once. And
now I have just gotten word that a letter was sent to you last week,
inviting you, as soon as you would consent, to come East, and take
charge of their new movement.

"Now, my dear fellow, don't say no."

"Here at last, then," said he, "is a door open. And
perhaps it is open soon enough. I have learned much in
my wanderings. And besides that, by the struggle and
sorrow I have gone through, I have learned that it is no
quick and easy thing to slip out of an old faith, and slip into
a new. So, instead of being hard and impatient toward
those just learning to walk after wearing shackles for years,
I trust I shall be tender and helpful in my rationalism."

The next day came the letter from New York, which he
read and pondered well, and determined to accept. But
how his heart still ached with the memory of the past ! He
was not a man to be crushed by it. He would fling it off,
and do a man's work, though with sadness in his soul.
"Fling it off ?" No : it would not be flung off. Neither
did he really desire that. It was the sunniest spot in all
his history. And he would remember it, though now and
henceforth he walked under a cloud. But he would treasure
it in the sacred privacy of his soul, and walk his way alone.
So perhaps he would be less trammelled in his work. At

any rate, whether it were well or ill, no present face, however fair, could for a moment seduce him from his tender loyalty to the remembered image.

On Thursday a large party gathered at the depot, and took special train for Mr. Harrold's villa. He was surprised to see so many.

"Why, Brimmer," said he, "I didn't suppose the whole town was going."

"Oh, this is nothing unusual! It is often many hundreds that make such a party. The grounds are so large, and the accommodations so ample, that there will seem to be no crowd. These men think nothing of spending a few thousands in this way on an afternoon. They charter a special train, and take a caterer from the city."

"At any rate, one will have a better chance to be alone, if he chooses. A crowd, next to the forest, is the place for solitude."

"But have I told you, Forrest, the occasion of this party?"

"I don't remember that you have."

"Well, then, get ready for a vision of loveliness. It's all in honor of a wonderful beauty that is visiting Harrold from the States, — daughter of an old schoolmate of his, or something of the sort. It is lucky for me that I'm married. But you, old fellow, may be in danger."

"I'm past all that," said he with an air of careless gayety; though he meant it with a sad emphasis down in his heart.

Meantime the cars were rushing down the valley, revealing, on either hand, glimpses of mountain and bay, of oakgrove and orchard, lovely nooks in the foot-hills, and villages across the water.

The most of the party were old acquaintances, and had been there before. So, when they reached the villa, without any formality they scattered rapidly over the grounds, each following the bent of his or her own fancy.

Mr. Forrest and Mr. Brimmer amused themselves a while in the billiard-room, and then strolled through the walks, and up in the tower that overlooked the place.

" Let's sit here, and talk a bit," said Mr. Forrest. " This must be a lovely way to live."

" Yes, when a man has made his pile. We ministers are in no special danger of doing that, I take it."

" No : I've never heard of ministers getting rich off their salaries. They sometimes marry a fortune, though they *do* preach that money is the root of all evil."

" Bah ! " exclaimed Mr. Brimmer, " what a humbug all that trash is ! Everybody knows money makes civilization. In the first ages there was some sense in the common talk about *worldliness*, and the separation of saints and sinners. But with the passing-away of paganism, and the growth of our modern life, there's no excuse for it. It's pretty hard to tell sometimes, whether there is more worldliness in the Church, or more godliness in the world.

" But what's the matter, Forrest? you look pale. You don't faint, do you ? "

Mr. Forrest did not answer, for he did not hear. He sat utterly lost and confounded at what he saw.

Mr. Brimmer looked in the direction in which he was

staring, and saw nothing more wonderful than a party of half a dozen people coming up the pathway toward the tower.

"Why don't you speak, Forrest?" exclaimed Mr. Brimmer. "Did you never see a group of people before? Why, that must be the stranger. But she *is* handsome though, isn't she?"

"Brimmer," exclaimed Mr. Forrest excitedly, springing to his feet, "I can't bear to meet *her* here. She's coming up the tower."

"Well, why not? I suppose you've met women before in your travels round the globe."

"Yes, and I've met *her* before; and that is why I can't."

But before he could explain, and find a way of escape, the party appeared, headed by Mr. Harrold. He grasped Mr. Brimmer by the hand, who then introduced him to Mr. Forrest. By this time all were up the stairs. The eyes of the two old-time lovers met. Margaret grew very white, and grasped the rail to support herself; and, as they were introduced, faltered out, addressing Mr. Harrold, —

"Yes, we have met before — at the East."

The friends noticed how strange and forced the greeting was, but were too courteous to mark it, and so make it more embarrassing. So, though they wondered what it meant, they tried to have all trace of it forgotten. After they had looked about a little, Mr. Harrold said, —

"Come, the whole party is going for a walk up the foot-hills. Let's join them."

Though it was torture for Mr. Forrest to be so near Miss Hartley, and not be able to ask her a thousand questions, — of past, of present, how she came here, and of other things more personal still, — and though he knew it must be equally hard for her, there seemed to be no way of escape.

As the merry company climbed the easy slope, and broke out at every fresh resting-place into new exclamations of delight at the widening view of the valley, the beauty of the shadows flitting in endless panorama over the sides and tops of the farther mountains, or the lengthening reach of bay with here and there the white of a sail, Mr. Forrest spoke in an undertone to Miss Hartley, and said, —

"For God's sake, Miss Hartley, don't say No. I *must* speak with you a moment."

"But how, here?" she replied.

"The company is gay and absorbed. They'll not miss us. May we not fall behind for a little?"

So, excusing herself to Mr. Harrold, she walked more slowly, and let the party precede her up the mountain.

"Here," said Mr. Forrest, "they're lost in the trees. May we not sit down under this oak?"

Though much constrained at first, they were soon speaking of the past in at least the tone of their old-time friendship. Mr. Forrest could not help noting how her eyes brightened, and the color came and went in her face, and that she seemed glad to be in his company once more. His heart leaped up with hope again; though he hardly dared ask what changes the years had brought, or whether the flight of time had left her free.

"Miss Hartley," said he, "am I forgiven beforehand for asking what perhaps I have no right to ask?"

"You have a right to ask all things you will."

"Has any other, then, gained the heaven from which I was cast out?"

"Mr. Forrest, did you once believe I loved you?"

"I did believe; and that one trust is the sunny spot in a life all dark beside."

"I do not think it is in me to love but once," she quietly replied.

He sprang to his feet, as he exclaimed, —

"Then, Madge, you " —

Just then she rose, laid her hand upon his arm, and said, —

"See, they are returning down the hill. We must join them."

But so changed was he in heart and appearance, that Mr. Brimmer exclaimed to him, as they linked arms, and the rest of the party sauntered on in irregular groups, —

"Why, Forrest, you look as if you'd seen a vision on the mountain. I don't think Moses' face shone brighter than yours."

"Banter away, old fellow. I can stand it now, for I have seen a vision."

"Have the astrologers and soothsayers of your court wisdom enough to interpret it?" said he. "If not, perhaps you'd better bring it to me for light."

"I think I can guess it. Nevertheless I think you can help me. I must stay here to-night."

"Well, here's an adventure. Is it about the beauty? I think I can fix it, whatever it is."

Mr. Forrest then told him his whole story; to which he listened as though it were a chapter out of a new novel. When he was done, he exclaimed, —

"But this is a queer old world. How things do come about! To run away round the world from a broken ring, and find it ready to be mended again, on the other side the globe!

"It's lucky I happened along. I am perfectly at home with Harrold. We'll both stay down to-night, and you shall have your opporunity. But she's a beauty though, Forrest. And here I am a minister. Lucky all round! Why, I'll marry you for half a price."

Mr. Brimmer seemed as happy for his friend as he did for himself.

The party returned to the city, and evening came. Mr. Brimmer explained affairs to Mr. Harrold; and so the two found themselves at liberty to be alone. As the sun set, and twilight came on, they went for a walk through the grounds, and entered an arbor overhung with grape-vines.

"O Madge!" he cried, "the horror of these three endless years!"

As he spoke, her own three years of waiting and heart-hunger crowded, a dismal procession, through her brain. She glanced up at his face; and then, as if fleeing from the pursuing phantoms of the past, with one word, — "Mark!" — half spoken, half sobbed, she rushed into his arms, and was folded close to his heart. He lifted her face towards his with one hand, while he clasped her with the other, and fairly rained his kisses on forehead, eyelid, and lips.

"But let us be glad, Madge," said he at last: "this crowning happiness pays for it all."

"O Mark, if you only knew what it cost me to even seem to be cruel to you!"

"It was an awful dream," said he; "but now we are awake and in heaven. Let us sit down and talk.

"And now, Madge," he continued, "though you are in my arms once more, and it would kill me to lose you again, I dare not ask you to lay your hand in mine, until I tell you what I am, and the path of life that is opening before me. I have wandered and studied and suffered, — as you know," said he, in a lower tone, — "since that dreadful night at Bluffton. But, religiously, I am only more and more convinced that God is the God of the whole earth, and of all religions. If I work again, it must be as one absolutely free to find God's truth any and every where, and speak it in all simplicity, but in all fearlessness."

"And I," she replied, "have greatly changed. I have tried to read and study, these years, and think I understand you now. You know through what a bitter struggle I clung to father and what I thought was duty. I'm thankful now that I was strong enough to suffer, and not to break his heart. But now *he* may look upon it as he was too old to look upon it here."

"I have just received this letter from New York." And here he unfolded and read it all aloud. "You see," he continued, "it is to be on the broadest basis. We shall not put in our creed any thing we do not know. It will be a church of and for this world, which is God's world. We shall only try to make men and women noble here; to build up and purify society; to build God's kingdom out of solid truths, on solid ground. We shall trust the future to Him who alone knows any thing about it. We shall have faiths and hopes and sentiments and poetry; but we shall try and remember that they are such, and not make our guesses and imaginations and wishes into sharp stones with which to strew the path of life, and make the feet bleed that travel over them.

"Can you find, Madge, any thing in a work like this, to engage your head, and enlist your heart?"

Saying which, he reached out toward her his hand. In this strong hand she quietly laid her own, as she replied, —

"In the dear old Bible story that mother read to me as a child, you have my answer: 'Whither thou goest I will go, and where thou lodgest I will lodge; thy people shall be my people, and thy God my God.'"

He drew her head down upon his shoulder, just as the yellow moon came up, looking through the vines, and shedding her tender benediction upon their happy love.